• THE RED DRAGON CHRONICLES •

THE LUCHAIR STONES

THE LUCHAIR STONES

ISABEL OGILVIE

The Luchair Stones
Book 1 in *The Red Dragon Chronicles*

ISBN: 978-1-907912-43-6

First published in the UK by Phoenix Yard Books Ltd, 2014.

Phoenix Yard Books
Phoenix Yard
65 King's Cross Road
London WC1X 9LW

www.phoenixyardbooks.com

Cover and inside artwork by Tomislav Tovik.

1 3 5 7 9 10 8 6 4 2

A catalogue record for this book is available from the British
Library

Dedications

To Jarryd, for sending Devlin to me.

To Natasha, Kayla, Jade and Chloe.
A little bit of Shay lives on in
each of you.

To Emma and Sue.
Thank you for your faith, patience and
perseverance.

GREAT ISLAND
Home of the
Three Kingdoms

Tainted Mountains
Northern Range
Gjufa Fjall
Hoorfrost
Lake of the Vanquished
Plateau
The Sentinel
Tainted Mountains
ange Territory
Culchan Territory
Sorrow
The Path of the Army
Mudflats
River of Promise
Plains of Abundance
The King's Highway
ROSEMERTA
Strait of Tremors
AARUSH
Aarush Castle

The Families Of

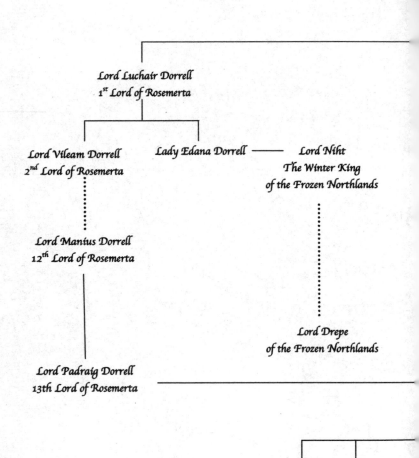

Isern the Blacksmith

Lord Luchair Dorrell
1ˢᵗ Lord of Rosemerta

Lord Vileam Dorrell
2ⁿᵈ Lord of Rosemerta

Lady Edana Dorrell ——— Lord Niht
The Winter King
of the Frozen Northlands

Lord Manius Dorrell
12ᵗʰ Lord of Rosemerta

Lord Drepe
of the Frozen Northlands

Lord Padraig Dorrell
13th Lord of Rosemerta

Aled   Siarl

The Great Island

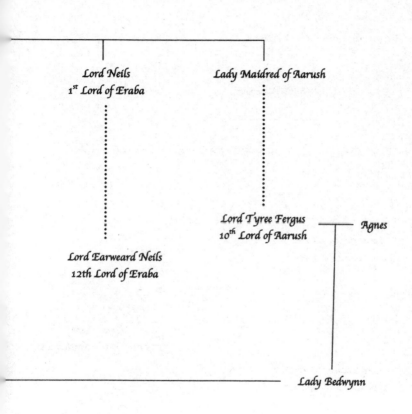

_____ Woman of the Forests

Lord Neils
1ˢᵗ Lord of Eraba

Lady Maidred of Aarush

Lord Tyree Fergus
10ᵗʰ Lord of Aarush — Agnes

Lord Earweard Neils
12th Lord of Eraba

Lady Bedwynn

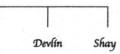

Devlin   Shay

PROLOGUE

Leaping fingers of flame filled the huge stone fireplace in the Great Hall of the cold, decaying citadel. A ghostly voice echoed through the dark chamber: 'Beware the child from the south.'

Drepe, Dark Lord of the Frozen Northlands, glared into the flaring hearth. His huge body shook with rage as he sat on his throne. Deep purple sapphires gleamed from the hollow sockets of a bleached skull embedded into the high-backed chair. One thick, calloused hand clutched a golden goblet; the other caressed the skeletal bones covering the arms of the throne.

He turned from the flames and stared into the eyes of the leather-clad man emerging from the shadows of the fire.

'Who is this child you warn me of? What do I have to fear from a mere child?'

Drepe's face contorted with rage as he glared at his spirit-caller. The flames receded into the bowels of the hearth. Drepe heaved himself up and threw the contents of his shining goblet into the fire. Filthy, curling hair fell in greasy strands around his face. Drops of wine dribbled through his long, matted beard.

'I fear no one from the south. There are none left to rise up and challenge me.'

A second figure, stooped and ghoulish, stepped out from the shadows. A tattered, red velvet cloak covered a dull, dirty breastplate of burnished copper. The knight's voice crackled as he spoke: 'Master, then we must throw the Stones. Only they can give you the full truth, foretell the future . . .' He glanced fearfully at his lord.

Drepe turned to the trembling man in the cloak and roared, 'Bring the Stones. Put to rest this falsehood my spirit-caller tells.'

The icy hall, lit only by the rising flames, sank into a deathly silence, broken only by the sound of restless hellhounds that trawled between long wooden tables, searching for scraps of food that were thrown onto the flagstone floor by black-clad figures. The thick dark fur of the beasts bristled in hackles along their spines. Spiked collars of silver reflected the golden flames, and their red eyes glowered in the darkness.

The knight shuffled from the chamber. Minutes later he returned, clutching a velvet bundle in his hand.

'Throw the Stones for me,' snarled the Dark Lord.

The knight withdrew a handful of dark blood-red stones. They were the size of cubed dice with strange inscriptions carved into their smooth sides. He flung them onto the rutted floor.

Drepe stared into the shadows of the leaping flames as the stones scattered around his leather boots. The knight looked down, drew back his head, and gasped.

'This cannot be. I will throw them again, my lord.'

Drepe pulled himself up to his full height and his dark shadow fell across the cowering figure. 'No!' he roared. 'Reveal to me the truth of the Stones or you will swing from Demon's Tree. Tell me now.'

The hellhounds fled to the dark corners of the hall as the knight shook with fear. 'The flames told the truth to your spirit-caller.' He pointed at the scattered stones. 'It is written here. There is one who remains in the south, and the Stones tell of this being a child. But a child does not wield a sword or lead an army. Fear not, my lord. You have defeated the army of the south. What can a child do without the protection of an army?'

'Fear? You dare to speak this word to your

master?' The Dark Lord pulled his hulking body from the Skull Throne and stared at the cowering knight. 'I do not need you to tell me that a child cannot defeat my forces. Return the Stones to the chest. Lock it tight, and bring me the key. Without the key, the stones can never be retrieved. Then you know what you must do.'

Drepe lowered himself onto the throne and his heavy boots lashed out at the hellhounds as they slunk from the shadows, seeking the warmth of the fire. A menacing calm fell over the dark citadel.

Moving close to the Dark Lord, the knight, clad in his tarnished armour, whispered, 'Yes, my lord. This child will not live long enough to reach the Stones.'

CHAPTER
1

'Devlin, you could at least try and fight me. It's not fair, just 'cause I'm a girl doesn't mean I can't fight you.'

Shay's voice echoed through the outer courtyard of the castle. A rare sliver of sun burst through the dark clouds, casting a circle of light around her tangle of red curls as she advanced on her opponent, thrusting a wooden sword at his chest.

Her cries did nothing to change the boy's

mood. Devlin threw down his wooden shield. A faded red dragon, carved into the face of the shield, stared up at him.

'What's the point of playing with wooden swords and shields when I'll never become a knight? What good is the Red Dragon now?' he said, as he kicked the shield across the dusty training yard. Shay glared at her brother, then she charged without warning, knocking the boy from his feet. As he lay on the hard ground, she held her wooden sword to his throat.

'You'll never be a warrior if you don't pay attention. When Father and our brothers come back, all they'll find is a whiny little boy, while I'll be ready for the tournaments to celebrate their triumphant return.'

Devlin, shaking with anger, sprang to his feet. Shay was two years younger, but many thought of his sister as the elder since she was already half a hand taller than him. Her red hair and athletic body, dressed in the breeches of a boy, contrasted with his smaller, slender frame and dark hair.

'They'll never return. They're dead!' he shouted. He turned on his heel, leaving a swirl of dust in his path, and headed across the empty training yard. Two harvests had passed since the outer yard had last bustled with the sounds of pages and squires, training with their knights, riding the wooden horse, practising with wooden shields and swords. Now only the pages remained as all the knights had gone, marching out with the army. Their squires had gone with them, too.

As Devlin passed beneath the arched entrance to the inner courtyard, Shay lunged, grabbing at his coarse woollen doublet. She knocked him down onto the hard cobblestones.

'Devlin, how can you say that?' she cried, pummelling her fists into his back. 'Of course they'll return. Mother and Uncle Caedmon have never given up, why should you? The army could return any day now, and if you give up practising, you won't be ready to begin your training to become a knight yourself.'

Devlin's face reddened. He rolled over and pushed his sister off his body, then stormed through the wide doorway leading into the round Red Tower and the Solar, where the family rooms of the royal family lay.

'Who's left to train me?' he shouted as Shay hurried behind him. 'Uncle Caedmon's old. All he can do is repeat the ancient stories. How will that help me?'

'Maybe you should listen and ask questions instead of sulking.'

Devlin scowled. 'You'll never understand. Go away, leave me alone.'

Shay followed him up the narrow winding stone steps leading to the Solar.

'Uncle Caedmon does his best,' she called out to his retreating back. 'He might be old, but he stands out in the courtyard for hours telling us what to do: how to hold our weapons; how to parry our swords. When the army returns I'll be ready and you'll still be riding the wooden horse.'

But Devlin wasn't listening. He rushed round

the final corner and collided with an old man in a hooded robe of heavy grey wool. The man's silver hair hung in two thick plaits across his sagging shoulders, and a sheathed sword hung from one side of a worn pigskin belt, opposite a small pouch of soft leather. Intricate carved, twisted knots covered both the scabbard and the pouch.

The old man sensed the boy's anger and frustration. 'Listen to your sister, Devlin,' he said, as Shay ran round too and into his outstretched arms. 'Try not to be so impatient. Your time is coming.'

'What do you mean, my time will come?' said Devlin, turning his back on both of them. 'The army rode out two harvests gone and we haven't heard anything of them since. They'll never return, and I'll never wear the armour of a knight.'

'Patience, Devlin, you must learn patience, and continue to practise. Your sister is proving herself to be a worthy opponent to you in your training,' replied Uncle Caedmon.

Shay's chest filled with pride, but Devlin stomped off, disappearing into the Solar and taking his scowl with him.

Colourful tapestries depicting generations of the royal family of Rosemerta hung from the high stone walls. In every panel, a red dragon hovered over the embroideries of castles and armies. The biggest tapestry, sewn by unknown hands, presented the revered story of Isern, the Blacksmith King of the Raedlands, and his founding of the three kingdoms of Rosemerta, Eraba and Aarush.

'Uncle Caedmon,' said Shay, 'read us again the story of the Stones. The Dark Lord may have stolen them away, but the army will surely come back with them.'

'How many times do you need to hear that old folktale?' Devlin said. 'It won't bring the army back.'

'If we give up they'll never return,' Shay said, turning away from him.

'Come here, children,' said Uncle Caedmon, as he settled into a chair next to the huge open fireplace. A fire blazed in a vain attempt to ward off the biting cold. He picked up a thick leather-bound tome.

'I know it's hard for you, Devlin, but you must believe me when I say that Rosemerta will once again become a land of peace and prosperity. The sun will shine again. The fields will be rich with crops once more. The army will return. Never forget your heritage. Listen to the words of your ancestors, passed along by the bards for generations past and future.'

As he opened the book and turned the yellowed pages, Shay nestled into the soft velvet cushions scattered by the hearth. She never tired of the old stories. Devlin leaned against a stone pillar, kicking at the edge of a rug with the toe of his boot and Caedmon began to read from the ancient manuscript.

The familiar words rolled over the children as

the old tale was retold:

In a distant land of ice and snow where the seasons of the sun were forsaken, a red streak hurtled through the night sky. A village blacksmith, on the plains of the lowlands south of the Tainted Mountains, watched as a great ball of flames crashed into the highest peak of these distant mountains.

That night a voice whispered in his dreams, 'Follow the flame.'

The blacksmith — Isern by name — left his home early next morning, following the path of the sun as it arced across the sky toward the mountains.

The abundance of the land and the rivers provided for him and, for ten days and ten nights, he travelled across the plains and into the mountains. He followed deep fjords carved from a thousand years of glaciers.

On the tenth night he entered the Realm of the Dark, on the edge of the Frozen Northlands. At the top of the Tainted Mountains, red cinders erupted, falling down as grey ash onto the frozen ground.

At the edge of a rocky ridge on the highest peak, he found a narrow gap in the face of a cliff. He scrambled inside, away from the biting wind, and followed a narrow path into a wide cave.

There, in the flickering light of his pitch-soaked torch, he saw a slumbering dragon. The creature was covered in red scales and smoke drifted into the stale air as it breathed. The dragon lifted one heavy eye and flames burst from its wide nostrils.

Strange inscriptions covered the walls of the cave and Isern glimpsed human bones and shattered weapons scattered across the hard, stony floor.

'Are you come to join them?'

Isern stepped back and looked around the cave.

'Who is here? Who speaks?' he said.

Isern looked into the eyes of the dragon and more words floated into his head.

'Answer me and you will get your answer.'

The dragon turned to the scattered bones.

'I will ask once more: have you come to join them?'

'I did not journey over mountains into this land

of ice and snow to join them in their restless sleep,'
Isern replied, then he told the dragon his story.

'I am only a blacksmith. The voices of the ancestors
spoke to me, telling me to follow the light as it
turned the night sky to day, and I have done as
they wished. I am here at their behest.'

'Then you are the one I have waited for.' The
dragon brushed its scaly tail into a dark corner of the
cave. A cloud of dirt swirled around the blacksmith.

The earth trembled beneath his feet and he felt
something hard against his leg. As the dirt settled he
looked down and saw a jagged red stone, the size
of a small boulder, at his feet.

'This is the treasure you seek; the treasure that
was sent from the skies. Take the Stone, and return
to your home so that I may return to mine.'

The dragon turned to face the carvings on the wall.

'Take these with you too. Pass my words to your
descendants and the land will prosper.'

'Great dragon,' the blacksmith said, 'how can I
share your words when I cannot read them?'

'There is no need for reading. Close your eyes.

They will know when to come to you. Now leave me. I grow weary and the mountains call me home.'

The blacksmith returned to his home, bearing with him the treasure of the dragon: the Raedstone. He was feted. The chieftains of the lowlands tribes bent their knees to him, naming him Isern, the Blacksmith King of the Raedlands, the land of the Dragon's Stone: one blessed by the dragon, to unite all under the red banner, to keep the people safe, to ensure their prosperity.

Isern knew what he must do. And so he forged the strongest and finest sword and shield he could from the Raedstone. When these had been fashioned, he carved six small stones from the remaining fragments. Each side he covered with symbols; the markings from the cave.

Years later, as King Isern lay on his deathbed, he divided the Raedlands between his sons — Luchair and Neils — and daughter, Maidred, and thus the three realms were formed: Rosemerta, Eraba and Aarush.

To Maidred in Aarush, he gave the Shield of the

Dragon, to give wisdom and to protect the people there from enemies.

To Neils in Eraba, he gave the Sword of the Dragon, to cut down any who challenged the peace of the land.

To Luchair in Rosemerta, he gave the Stones of the Dragon, the truth-tellers, to protect and provide. Never forget their power,' Isern said. 'Guard them and they will guide and protect you, and those who follow, from the coming darkness.'

His last gift to his children was a parchment written in his own hand.

'These words were passed to me by the Great Dragon,' he said.

They looked at the verse.

'What does this mean?' Luchair asked.

'Luchair, you are my eldest. A day will come for your descendants when these words will ring true.'

Then Isern turned his face from his children and drew his last breath.

Devlin knew the story by heart. The Luchair Stones, the Stones of Rosemerta, had been carved from the ancient Raedstone. The seasons turned and the harvests were bountiful, providing enough to feed the three lands. The River of Hope flowed through the wide fertile plains of Rosemerta, bringing fresh clear water down from the mountains. Crops grew in abundance. The words of King Isern were not forgotten. The Stones had sat in the fields through the nights of the Seeding festivals every year, unguarded... for who could have imagined any risk?

CHAPTER
2

The man lay beneath a dying oak. The branches were gnarled and bare. He remembered the tree, had climbed it, hidden in the thick leaves, throwing its fruit at his brothers, laughing.

He gulped down the last drops of water from his flask. Greasy locks of black hair fell around his shoulders. He stood, looking down at his clothes – the tattered cloak and the tarnished breastplate – and he wondered if they would know him. He had missed his people, but he owed his duty to another now.

Two harvests had passed since he had left his home, but the time had come. He was returning. He thrust his hand into the satchel hanging at his side and touched the parchment. Then he looked at the red walls of Rosemerta Castle. When he had last seen these walls they had shimmered in the sunshine, like the burnished copper armour of a knight of Rosemerta. Now they were dark and gloomy beneath the rolling shadows of heavy black clouds.

He watched a lone guard pacing the battlement above the gatehouse. The heavy wooden gates were closed to outsiders. A movement caught his eye. A girl child could be seen through an archer's opening in a corner tower. Then a black-haired boy leaned out.

★★★★★

The story over, Devlin kicked at a pillar, pulled his cloak around his body and made his way across the room toward the closed door.

'Where are you going?' Shay called, jumping up from the cushions and chasing him out through the door. She grabbed at his cloak.

'Outside,' he said, wrenching the cloth from her hands. 'You might believe they're coming back, but I don't. Look.' He pointed through the window at the fields. 'Another winter is almost here. The frosts are thicker than last year, the wind is colder. Where are the crops? If the Stones were coming home, the crops would be ready for harvest now.' He grabbed the brass handle, and flung the Solar door open.

His footsteps echoed on the spiralling stairs and he felt Shay's eyes on him as he stormed across the courtyard, to the nearest watchtower. He raced up the stairwell, his leather boots pounding on the sandstone steps, until he reached the top landing where he leaned out through a narrow archer's opening in the thick wall.

The wind whipped him around the face, and Devlin pulled up the hood of his cloak, only for the wind to blow it away again. He looked out across the low outer wall of the castle.

The fields were brown, the ground hard and cracked. Corn withered on the stalk. The harvest had been abandoned before it could begin. It was nothing like it had been on that terrible day over two years ago, Devlin thought. He remembered working side by side with his father, brothers, knights and crofters, planting the seeds for the summer harvest. The day had been long and hot and they had rested in the shade of the apple grove, drinking cool water from the stream, plucking shiny red apples from the trees.

The sky had turned dark as a wall of black riders descended from a nearby hill, battering their way through the open fields, the hooves of their rearing battle horses destroying the newly planted seeds. A huge man, clad in black armour and wearing a shiny ebony helm forged in the shape of a human skull, led his army on a coal-black warhorse. Smoke poured from the beast's nostrils, and sparks rose from its iron-clad hooves. The man wheeled the grunting horse round the red granite platform in the middle of the fields, reached down with a mail-clad fist, and snatched up the circle of six red stones.

As a horn sounded from the hilltop, the black riders reeled in their mounts and followed their master back across the devastated fields.

Drepe had stolen the Stones!

A week of frenzied activity had followed before the army rode out in pursuit of the Dark Lord, in search of the Luchair Stones. Devlin had watched from the battlement above the gatehouse as his father, Lord Padraig, and his brothers, Aled and Siarl, rode out at the head of the army. He stood with his mother – the Lady Bedwynn – and his sister Shay, as the knights rode out in rows of four, their dragon breastplates dazzling in the sunlight. They were followed by a thousand men-at-arms. Their banners, which showed the Red Dragon encircled by six red stones, fluttered in the breeze atop their tall spears. Women threw flowers at the prancing hooves of the horses, children chased each other through the lines of soldiers, and old men too frail to join the knights lamented their age. Thunderous cheers rose in chorus with a hundred horses' hooves clattering across the cobblestones.

For months, all through the long cold winter, the people waited for news. Summer passed. The women and children planted the autumn crop in the hard land, danced around the seeding fires, and waited for the rains to come. Another long, cold winter covered the land, and once again the rains failed.

Another summer approached with no crop to harvest, no fires to dance around, and a harsh winter looming. The River of Hope had dried to a trickle, the plains nothing now but dust and withered crops as far as Devlin could see. There were few people about. But as he looked down from the tower, he noticed a ragged man staggering along the rough uneven track, and then collapsing at the closed gates to the castle.

'Halt, stranger,' the sentry shouted. 'Announce your name and your intentions.'

'News. I have news of Lord Padraig,' the man gasped, pulling his cloak across his lean body just after Devlin thought he'd glimpsed a Dragon breastplate.

'How can I trust you?' called the sentry. 'Prove yourself.'

'The message must be passed directly to the Lady Bedwynn. Lord Padraig commanded that I speak only to the Lady.'

'You cannot enter the castle until I have permission to open the gates,' called the sentry.

The shouts brought people from all corners of the castle. Caedmon was amongst the first to come rushing from the inner bailey of the castle. He climbed the stone steps to the battlements with an agility that gave lie to his age. Standing next to the sentry, he looked down on the dirty, unkempt figure. A tingling feeling spread through Caedmon's old bones.

'Open the gates!' he ordered.

'But, my lord, how do we know he has not been sent by the Dark Lord?' said the sentry.

'It is a risk we must take. We have heard nothing since the army rode out. This may be the news we have waited so long for.'

The sentry called down to the guards standing at the base of the gates, 'Lord Caedmon has spoken. Unbolt the gates.'

The great wooden gates creaked slowly open on their giant brass hinges and the stranger tumbled through, barely able to stand as he gasped, 'Take me to the Lady. I must deliver my message to the Lady Bedwynn and to no one else. My liege, Lord Padraig, has entrusted me to speak to no one else.'

Caedmon stepped forward. 'Follow me. I will take you to the Lady.'

The stranger lurched unsteadily into the Great Hall of the castle.

Bedwynn gasped, for beneath the grime she had glimpsed the faded image of the Red Dragon on the breastplate over the man's soiled and torn tunic.

The stranger knelt before the Lady, and Devlin and Shay, having joined the commotion, stood on either side of their mother. People were crowding into the hall, anxious to hear of any news – good or bad.

'I am the last survivor of our once-great army,' the man gasped. 'A messenger with news you will not wish to hear. We have been defeated. Our army is broken. The Dark Lord has frozen them deep inside a great ice wall rising from the frozen lake surrounding his citadel. The very last order I received from Lord Padraig was that I should find my way back to Rosemerta and deliver the news. All is lost. The Stones will never return to Rosemerta, and our land remains condemned to the darkness.' He looked up at Bedwynn and whispered, almost as if to himself, 'Do you not know me, Mother?' Then he collapsed at her feet, as if the effort of speaking had drained the very life from him.

The Lady looked down on the ragged figure. Something about this man – the black hair and dark eyes – reminded her of her sons, but her sons had been tall and strong, like their father. This poor wretch held no more resemblance than the colour of his hair and eyes.

'Water, bring water for this poor man,' she called to a nearby servant.

Water was brought to the stranger's lips and he rose himself awkwardly on to his knees again.

Caedmon stepped forward and knelt before his niece. 'This cannot be true, my lady. We must never give up.'

Caedmon, the Lady's uncle, was her closest advisor. He had travelled to Rosemerta with his niece when she had wed Padraig. Too old now to ride out with the army, he had remained to care for his niece and her remaining children, but Caedmon had always believed that the army would return triumphant from the battle. Now he turned to the stranger and spoke.

'Tell me more. How can we trust you? What evidence do you bring to prove you have been sent by Lord Padraig?' he said. 'How do we know that you have not been sent by Drepe to trick us into sending our last remaining men?'

'I am the messenger sent by my father, Lord Padraig,' the man said as he gulped down a tumbler of cold water. 'I am to pass on this message and map to my mother, and to no one else.'

Bedwynn's eyes widened before squinting harder at the wreck of the man in front of her. *Aled?* No, for the comparison between her first born and the figure in front of her was too great. Shorter in stature, it had to be, but it couldn't be...

'Siarl? My son Siarl...' The words broke the silence as Bedwynn sank to her knees and embraced him. Tears rolled down her face. 'You have returned from the dead. But what have they done to you?'

'Yes, Mother, I have returned, but first you must read my father's words.' Siarl held a worn leather pouch in his outstretched hand, the outline of the Red Dragon barely visible on the frayed flap.

Bedwynn reached out, took the pouch from the gnarled hands and opened it. Two pieces of crumpled parchment fell to the ground, and she bent to pick them up: a map and a message. As she read the words, Bedwynn gasped and held her hand to her throat:

My dearest Bedwynn,

If this message reaches you, then you will know our army has been overcome. But all is not lost. The map will lead the Chosen One to the Frozen Northlands. There is still time. Siarl will lead the way.

The army can only return with the Stones if the child, our only hope, is sent to cross the mountains. Promise me you will do this.

Padraig.

Bedwynn stood transfixed by the note in her

hand, at Padraig's familiar handwriting.

'No, this cannot be true. Padraig cannot expect a mere boy to be the Chosen One. He is too young! I cannot lose another son to the Dark Lord. Why should the Chosen One not be Siarl or Aled?'

She looked at her son Siarl, now returned from the dead.

Caedmon stood at her side. He took the note and map from her shaking hands. 'If Siarl was meant to be the one, he would have returned with the army, but he has not. He is only a messenger.'

'No, Uncle, Padraig asks too much,' Bedwynn murmured. 'I have already lost my husband and eldest son. I do not wish to sacrifice another son to Drepe.'

'My lady,' Caedmon said softly. 'The time has come. The boy is ready. He is the one.'

Even as Caedmon whispered the words, Bedwynn knew he was right. Holding herself proudly, she spoke to the assembled crowd.

'My brave son, Siarl, has returned with news of the army, sent by his father, Lord Padraig. Devlin will leave Rosemerta with his brother Siarl as soon as preparations can be made for the journey. My sons will follow the map to the Ice Citadel and retrieve the Stones.'

A gasp rippled through the crowded hall. *How could this be?* they thought. *He is only a boy.*

What hope could a thirteen-year-old boy have against an enemy that had defeated the largest army ever assembled in the land of Rosemerta?

CHAPTER 3

Bedwynn turned from the crowd, clutching the leather pouch to her chest. Her long crimson gown swept across the dark flagstones as she left the Great Hall. Caedmon followed, supporting a limping Siarl. Shay ran ahead, racing up the spiralling stone steps leading to the Solar. Devlin lingered in the hall.

'Are you coming?' Shay called to Devlin. 'Uncle Caedmon is moving faster than you!'

Devlin trailed behind, trying to make sense of

everything that had just happened. Unanswered questions swirled in his head as he pushed at the door of the Solar. He loved this room: the curved walls seemed to wrap around him and he would spend hours on the wide window seat, looking out over the sweeping plains to the low foothills of the distant mountains. On rare days when the clouds lifted, he could see the snowy peaks, and he imagined his father leading the victorious army home. Aled and Siarl would be with him, the Dragon banner waving proudly at their side. Not that he would ever admit it to his sister.

'Come in,' Caedmon said, jolting Devlin from his thoughts. 'Join us. Your mother wishes to talk with you.'

Bedwynn stood with her back to the door, gazing at a large wall hanging. The map lay on the pitted surface of an oak table, held in place by heavy brass candlesticks. Thick drapes covered the window and tallow candles flickered, casting long shadows across the room. Shay stood at her mother's side, still wearing her boy's breeches and leather vest.

Devlin looked at the tapestry hanging from a thick brass rod on the pink granite wall. This was the first panel of Rosemerta. The remaining six panels hung in the Great Hall.

The Solar panel depicted the first Lord of Rosemerta, Luchair, eldest son of King Isern. Two children sat at his feet, Villeam and his twin sister Edana. Rosemerta Castle sat on the cliff, looking over the calm waters of the harbour. Ships with colourful sails bearing the symbols of distant lands filled the quay. Exotic goods filled their holds: silks as soft and colourful as the flowers in the castle gardens; ceramic pots filled with sweet-smelling spices; sparkling jewels to grace a lady's throat.

Devlin thought back to the scene he'd been staring at moments before Siarl returned. Now only bony cattle and matted flyblown sheep grazed on dusty brown stubble. Apple and pear trees were bare of fruit, and ships with tattered sails sat idle in the dock.

Bedwynn turned to face Devlin and he looked into his mother's green eyes, at the worry in her face and the grey in her hair. In the tapestry in the Great Hall in which she appeared, his mother was a young, smiling bride with flowing red curls.

'Mother, Uncle, what is happening?' Devlin didn't know what they wanted of him. He pointed at the map on the table.

It showed a line of mountains in the north, separating the three lands from the Frozen Northlands. Swathes of forests, meandering rivers and streams criss-crossed the land, while a strip of desert to the west separated Eraba from Rosemerta. To the east, beyond the Strait of Tremors, lay the island of Aarush. The River of Hope flowed down from the Tainted Mountains, into the Bay of Rosemerta.

Devlin had spent hours pouring over maps, daydreaming of the faraway lands represented by line and colour. He knew these familiar countries and their boundary markings like the lines on his own hands. But there were markings on this map he'd seen on no other.

'What are these?' Devlin said as his finger traced the strange markings: circles within circles, stars and arrows following the path of the river, edging along the desert and into the mountains.

'Villages,' Siarl said, stepping in from the shadows of the room, 'and waterholes. Safe camping places for our journey; signposts.'

'What am I to tell Devlin?' Bedwynn said, looking at Caedmon. 'I never stopped believing my husband would return victorious with my sons, leading our army through the castle gates.'

'I know you are afraid, but this is what Devlin has trained for,' Caedmon replied. 'We appealed to our deities for their safe return, but now this terrible news has come to us. Padraig has sent his message. Siarl has returned to us. The map marks the way. Padraig would never have sent this message if he did not think the boy was ready.'

Devlin stepped between his mother and uncle.

'I am here too. I can hear you. What is it? What am I supposed to do?' His voice wavered.

Bedwynn looked at him. She knew the time had come, and her youngest son must know the truth.

'We had always believed the army would return to Rosemerta with the Stones,' she said, 'but as the seasons passed by with no news we feared the worst. For too long we dismissed the words of our great ancestor, Isern, warning us that this time would come. He told us of a child who would save us from the Dark. "The Chosen One". The Dark is here, but Siarl has been returned to us and now we can hope again.'

'What are you talking about? What ancient words? What child?' Devlin said, turning to his uncle. 'I have read the manuscripts; I know the history of the three lands, and there was no warning, no mention of a child.' He waved his arm at the leather-bound manuscripts filling the shelves of the Solar. 'The history of the

Raedlands, of Rosemerta, is in these. How many times have you told us the stories of our past, Uncle? Now you tell me this,' he said. 'Show me the words.'

'I have them,' Caedmon said, taken back by the intensity in Devlin's voice. 'They were written down two thousand years ago. But our army was strong. How could a child ever be needed to save us? As the years passed, we chose to forget these words of Isern and brought disaster upon ourselves. Now your brother has returned with your father's message to remind us.'

He turned from Devlin and stepped over to a dusty shelf filled with thick books. As he pulled down three volumes, he reached in and ran his fingers along the edge of a stone block in the wall. The stone slid back and Devlin watched as his uncle reached in and pulled out a rolled parchment tied with a leather thong.

'What is it?' Devlin and Shay called out together as they gathered around the old man.

Caedmon unrolled the parchment and turned

to face the children.

'Read it, Uncle,' Shay said, tugging at the sleeve of his jacket.

The old man looked at Bedwynn.

She nodded and turned to Devlin. 'The time has come. Listen.'

Caedmon spoke slowly, the words flowed softly:

> '*When the land is cold and dark,*
> *When all is lost,*
> *One will come, a child of the*
> *blacksmith's blood,*
> *To rise up and challenge the Darkness,*
> *To journey into the ice and fire,*
> *Where—*'

His voice trailed off as he placed the parchment on the table next to the map.

'But why didn't you tell me? What does it mean? It's not even finished.' Devlin felt his blood rising in his body as the realisation of what his mother had announced to the court set in.

'I had a right to know. How do you even know it's me? Why did you keep it hidden?' He picked up the parchment and fingered the torn edge where the words ended. 'What about the rest? Maybe it says something more about Siarl?'

Bedwynn stepped forward and put her arm round Devlin's shoulder. 'No,' she said. Her voice trembled and her hands shook. 'It does not refer to Siarl. The rest of the message has disappeared. I have never seen it, but when the army marched out I believed the child would be one of your brothers. Aled was seventeen, Siarl sixteen when they left – both still children to me,' she added. Tears glistened in her eyes.

'Siarl has returned only to show you the way,' said Caedmon, holding out the crumpled map. 'Your brother will lead you north. He is a brave man and he will protect you from danger. If the fear comes, think of the Blacksmith King, for his strength is in you.'

As Shay listened she grew angry. No one was mentioning her. She was as brave as Devlin, and she too had learned the ways of a young warrior, training alongside her brother, for she had never been interested in learning the arts the other girls seemed to enjoy so much. She found it impossible to sit still and work at her embroidery when Devlin was training in the courtyard below, so she had gone out to join him. The message spoke of a child, not a boy. Why shouldn't that child be her?

'What about me?' she shouted. 'How do you know the child of the Stones is Devlin? It could be me!' Her face was now as red as her hair.

'Of course it's me. I'm a boy, you're a girl,' Devlin said.

Shay charged. Caedmon grabbed the back of her jerkin as she launched at Devlin.

'That's enough from both of you,' he said. 'There is no more to be said. Tomorrow Devlin will begin to prepare for the journey.'

Shay glared at Devlin as she lowered her fists, then turned on her heel and stomped out of the room.

Next morning, Bedwynn left the Solar and stood on the steps outside the Great Hall to address her people. She fingered a necklace of coloured stones as she looked into anxious faces.

'You have already heard. Yesterday, news of our army arrived. My son Siarl has returned safely to his home and he bears a message from Lord Padraig.'

She turned to her son. Siarl was no longer dressed in rags. He wore a copper helm with the visor raised, showing his dark eyes. Thick black hair fell around his shoulders and his beard was neatly trimmed. The Red Dragon blazed from his black tunic, but his bare hands still betrayed his scaly skin.

'Siarl, my beloved son, your father has charged you with the duty of escorting your brother Devlin on his journey. You will protect him and keep him from harm. He must cross the threshold of the citadel of Drepe. The Dark Lord will not be expecting a boy this young. Devlin carries with him a power given to our ancestor, the Blacksmith King. Devlin must free the army from their ice-bound prison and we must finally defeat the forces of evil.'

Siarl looked first at Devlin and then his mother. 'I shall guard my brother with my life, my lady mother,' he replied in a deep, slow voice.

Caedmon stepped forward and spoke.

'Preparations for the journey will begin today. Siarl and Devlin will be ready to leave on the sixth rising of the morning sun from this day.'

The people cheered and children ran joyously through the crowd, lifting the spirits of all. Shay stood in the shadows. She watched silently as her uncle led Devlin back to the training yard.

'You must spend this time wisely,' she heard him say to Devlin. 'Siarl will protect you, but you must continue to practise your swordplay and archery until the sixth rising.'

'Uncle,' Devlin said, 'what if the words are wrong? I'm only a boy.'

The dark clouds cast long shadows from the castle walls across the courtyard. Shay sat huddled in the cold, her arms wrapped tightly round her knees. She was angry; angry that no one had listened to her. A hand stroked her shoulder and she felt the caress of soft velvet on her cheek.

'It is time we spoke.'

Shay jumped up and looked into her mother's eyes. People said she had her mother's eyes, green with flecks of gold. And these eyes were looking at her now in a new way; a way that spoke of secrets.

That evening Devlin sat alone in the Solar listening to the sounds of celebration coming from the Great Hall beneath the room. He pulled back the heavy woollen drapes and stared out into the darkness shrouding the plains. Clouds covered the moonless sky.

Later he slipped down to the stables.

'Cato,' he said as his horse nuzzled his shoulder, 'I'm not ready. I don't care what the words say. I don't know what is expected of me. I'm afraid, and you're the only one I can tell.'

The big brown eyes of the bay gelding looked at the boy. They seemed to say, 'You will be safe with me.'

Devlin returned to his room. Tomorrow he would begin the preparations for a journey into the unknown. *I am a son of Rosemerta*, he told himself, even as he questioned his strength. *I must not show my fears.*

Each day was a bustle of activity. The journey across the plains would be dangerous and food supplies would be hard to come by. Perhaps there would be some struggling crops on a tired farm, or a village well that held fresh water from underground springs. Precious meat, smoked and salted to preserve it for the journey, was packed into saddlebags, leather water bags were filled and warm clothes packed.

Hour after hour, Devlin practised his archery and swordplay with his brother. The wooden sword was now replaced by a sword of black Erabean iron, given to him by his uncle the morning after Siarl's return.

'I have something for you,' Caedmon had said, as Devlin prepared to practise with the wooden sword as usual. 'This belonged to Aled when he was your age. It was his first true sword. Now it is yours.' He held out a black sword half the length of a knight's weapon.

Devlin knew that only the lords of the Three Lands, and their sons, were entitled to carry swords forged from the rare black ore of the mines of Eraba and his chest swelled with pride as he held the weapon.

That night he dreamed of his brothers. Aled and Siarl were with him in the training yard...

'Come, Devlin,' said Aled. 'Today we will teach you the skills of the archer.' He presented the small boy with a bow specially made to fit his small hands. The arrows, tipped with bright-coloured feathers, sat inside a leather quiver, ready to sling across his slender shoulders. Devlin felt strong and proud. Now he was no longer treated as a baby but he was training with his brothers.

Siarl unexpectedly swung his sword at Aled, knocking him from his feet and onto the hard ground.

'Brother, admit defeat,' cried Siarl. 'I have you at my mercy.' He held his sword high above his head as if he were ready to thrust it into his brother's chest. His dark eyes blazed with anger.

'It is only a game, Siarl. Put down the sword. You are frightening Devlin,' said Aled, rising to his feet as he pulled his own sword from the scabbard hanging from his belt; the black sword Devlin now wielded.

Siarl slowly lowered his sword and glared at his brothers. 'One day it will not be a game,' he snarled, storming from the training yard.

'Poor Siarl,' said Aled, sheathing the sword of black iron. 'I fear he will never accept his role as my younger brother. He believes he should be the one chosen to lead our people one day.'

'But, Aled, Father leads our people. That is how it has always been. How could Siarl believe that he could lead us?'

Aled looked down at his young brother. 'Don't worry about Siarl, little brother. You are right; Father will always be here to protect us.'

Someone was shaking Devlin's shoulder. His brothers faded away.

'No!' he cried. 'Come back. I need you.'

'Devlin, wake up. You're having a bad dream.'

He heard his mother's gentle voice call from somewhere in the distance. He opened his eyes. and she stood over him.

'It is time. Siarl waits.'

The inner courtyard bustled with activity. A stableboy tightened the strap on Cato's girth. Siarl was seated on a coal-black stallion. A smaller pack horse was laden with supplies for the journey, and roped to the stallion.

Devlin reached up to the pommel and climbed onto Cato. He patted the horse's neck as he settled into the saddle.

Siarl followed on his stallion. He wore a copper breastplate over a shirt of mail. His long black hair hung in their six plaits, splaying out from beneath his helm and falling around his narrow shoulders. An iron sword, sheathed in a leather scabbard, hung at his side and a circular shield of bronze was strapped across his back. The black beast snorted and stamped.

'Time to go, boy,' Siarl said from beneath the closed visor. His horse reared up, forcing his rider to pull tightly on the reins. 'He doesn't like that horse of yours. Make sure you keep him away. I won't be responsible for what might happen,' he added, pulling his black cloak around his body.

Devlin looked ahead as the inner courtyard gates swung open. Siarl pressed his spurs into the side of the stallion and led Devlin through the arched gateway, into the outer courtyard. Devlin looked up to the battlement where his mother and uncle stood. As he and Siarl pulled their horses to a halt so they could call out their final farewells they heard the metallic clip of a horse behind them.

Devlin turned in his saddle. 'What are you doing here?' he said, looking at Shay.

She rode her white mare, Emilia, and packed bags hung from her saddle. Like Devlin she wore leather breeches and a jerkin, and a leather scabbard hung from one side of her belt, a sword hilt peeking out from the top. A cloth bag hung from the other side. A copper shield slung across her back was hidden beneath the folds of her green hooded cloak.

Siarl looked up to where his mother stood with Caedmon. 'Why is the girl here, Mother? Call her back,' he growled.

'No, Siarl. Shay will help you,' Bedwynn replied.

'What do you mean? How can she help?' Devlin said.

'Yes,' Siarl said, as he lifted his visor and stared at his mother, 'do tell.'

Caedmon shifted uncomfortably on his feet. He had counselled Bedwynn against sending the girl, but she had remained steadfast.

'You will thank me by the end of your journey. I know you cannot see it now, but in time you will.' Bedwynn's voice wavered. 'Care for each other. We will await your safe return.'

CHAPTER
4

Loud shouts rose up and echoed around the stone walls of the castle. Every window and arrow slit showed the Red Dragon, rearing boldly from golden banners fluttering in the breeze. The path leading to the outer courtyard was lined with castle workers: cooks in their stained aprons; maids and kitchen hands; all waiting for the riders.

Devlin stared ahead, afraid to look up and meet his mother's gaze. She had slipped a small parchment into the inside pocket of his padded woollen jerkin. 'For your father,' she had said. He could still feel her hands closing the last bronze button. His jerkin, dark as Cato's mane, displayed the badge of the Red Dragon. A strap of thick braided twine held his leather quiver across his back, and a bow of red oak with a sheaf of feathered arrows rose above his dark head, like a spiked helmet. A cloak of russet wool lay rolled up across Cato's saddle.

The portcullis gates lifted. The three rode side by side, Devlin and Shay on Cato and Emilia, both at one side of the black stallion, with the pack horse following behind. The drawbridge echoed with the clattering hooves of the animals.

Devlin was lost in thought. His stomach churned. Ahead lay the dry plains, the river crossing and the distant snow-tipped mountains. He knew that the Frozen Northlands lay beyond the mountains, as did the icy prison of Rosemerta's army.

He turned and raised his hand in a final silent farewell to his mother as she turned, stepping through the doorway of the tower. Their farewells had been said last night in the privacy of the Solar, and Devlin feared that he would turn Cato round for the safety of the castle if he spoke to his mother now. His last words to her had been something he found hard.

He knew he now had to be brave, so he hid his fears as he urged Cato out through the wide gates. The land beyond the castle walls was brown and barren and Devlin looked across the fields and recalled the stories of the old people: of the years when the seasons followed each other, and abundant harvests had filled the storehouses of Rosemerta and the holds of ships returning to Eraba and Aarush.

'Cheer up.' Shay leaned across her saddle and smiled mischievously at Devlin. 'If you get into trouble I can help you.'

Devlin ignored her and trotted Cato up next to the stallion.

'Why would Mother send Shay?' he asked Siarl. 'The message didn't say anything about two children. It's not right."

'And you think I'm happy?' Siarl said without turning, his eyes staring into the distance.

'You had to do this, didn't you?' Devlin shouted back at his sister. 'You couldn't stay behind. You're jealous that I'm a proper boy. You should have stayed behind. You heard what Mother and Uncle Caedmon said. I've been chosen, not you. Turn around and go home – now!'

'Well, well,' said the messenger. 'My little brother has spirit, after all.'

'I'm staying,' Shay said, glaring at Siarl. 'You can't send me home. I have Mother's blessing. Anyway, the story spoke of a child. They didn't say anything about a boy or girl. How do you know it's not me?'

'Listen to Devlin.' Siarl's voice bellowed. 'He is right. Return while you still can.'

'No,' she replied defiantly, pulling her short

sword from its scabbard and pointing it at her brothers. 'I am coming with you. Devlin, did you really think you could leave me behind? Lord Padraig is my father too. I can help.'

'How? With scissors and pins? Put away that toy,' Siarl said.

'I have this sword. And I can use a bow and arrow as well as you. If you try to stop me I'll just follow you,' Shay said, thrusting her sword into its scabbard and gripping Emilia's reins firmly as she returned Siarl's glare.

'I've got enough to do with looking after one child. Now I have to babysit two. Has Mother lost her wits?' Siarl made little effort to mask his contempt.

Shay kicked Emilia's flanks and trotted ahead of her brothers. She turned in her saddle. 'Well? Are you coming, or do I have to do this myself?'

A cold wind swirled and twisted around the horses, leaving a cloud of brown dust in their wake. Hungry villagers with hollow eyes stared from doorways. Scrawny dogs fought over scraps, and bony chickens scratched in the dirt. Devlin scanned the dismal landscape and thought about the journey ahead. He had studied the map under the guidance of Caedmon. He knew the River of Promise lay on the far side of the low hills, several days' travel beyond the village.

The ride was long and hard. Devlin followed silently behind his brother, ignoring Shay's presence. He still could not believe his mother would allow her to come. The riders ate in the saddle, resting only to graze their horses. At night, they took shelter in abandoned homesteads, sleeping on the cold ground, wrapped in their cloaks. Since they had left the sanctuary of the castle, Siarl had barely spoken, other than to give directions or to indicate where to stop or when to eat.

On the third day they passed through Obar, a tiny abandoned settlement on the far side of the windswept plain. Dark clouds hovered over the distant mountains as they rode in single file along the rutted track through the village.

Siarl led, followed by Devlin. Shay lingered behind, still angry. On the far edge of the village Siarl reeled his horse round and pulled up his visor. Pitch-black eyes glared out from the copper helmet.

'Night is falling quickly,' he said. 'Hurry, or you'll be feed for wild dogs.' His words were harsh, his stare penetrating.

Shay pulled up Emilia and made to dismount.

'What are you doing, girl?' Siarl said.

'We could spend the night here,' she said. 'Look over there, that stable still has its roof and it's cold.'

'We need to cross the River of Promise before the dark falls,' Siarl continued, ignoring her as if she had never spoken. 'Now move your animal.'

Devlin was jolted by his tone. He looked at the sky; the night wasn't far behind them. The last thing he wanted to do was let Siarl think he was siding with Shay, so he tried to make the words come out right. 'Will we make camp on the other side of the river?' he asked as he drew Cato up level with the black stallion.

'The crossing will be dangerous. With less talk we may make camp tonight on the far side of the river,' his brother said, in a voice that made it clear he would not tolerate any further discussion.

In the days before they had left the castle Siarl had been friendly, but reserved. Now he was cold and distant, making it clear he expected them to follow unquestionably. Devlin lowered his head and bit his lip, then gently dug his heels in Cato's flanks and hurried to keep pace with the stallion. Shay rode off to one side, refusing to look at her brothers.

The journey continued once again in silence. Brittle brown grasslands crowded in on them, and heavy grey clouds continued to cover the mountain peaks. Lightning lit up the black sky, and the earth rumbled beneath them. Devlin had glimpsed these storms across the plains before, and each time he'd hoped they would deliver the much-needed rain that never came to Rosemerta.

As they climbed the first hill he felt more alone than ever as he stared at his brother's back. Had he looked behind him, Devlin would have known Shay had been urging Emilia ever so slightly forward and had closed the gap between them.

Siarl held up his hand, pulling tightly at the reins of his straining horse. 'The river is just beyond the next hill. Push your horses harder if you want to cross before dark.' He kicked the sweat-stained flanks of the stallion as he charged up a narrow track.

Devlin sat on Cato with his feet firmly planted in the stirrups of the saddle and urged his horse up the steep incline.

'Come on, Cato. We are nearly there,' Devlin said to his panting horse.

Reaching the top of the hill, Devlin gazed down at the River of Promise. He saw a dry riverbed gouged out of a steep ravine. This was not what he had expected. A river should flow with water, surely. The River of Promise of the tapestries had flowed through a green valley. Despite Rosemerta's troubles, when Devlin looked at all those maps he had assumed the land beyond Rosemerta still held true to the legends and paintings. What a foolish child he was. But why would Drepe curse these lands? Devlin realised how little he knew about the world beyond Rosemerta, which made him cross and sad at the same time.

Cato reared up his head, looking into the distance. His ears were pinned forward and he pulled at the reins.

'It's the storm,' Siarl said. 'Look to the mountains. We need to be across the river before the storm.'

Devlin peered into the distance. 'Is that fog on the mountain?' he asked.

'You'll find out soon enough,' replied Siarl. Now get moving, both of you.'

Devlin leaned down and patted Cato's flank.

'It's all right,' he said. 'We're almost there.'

'Keep that animal under control. It's enough that I have to keep watch over children without worrying about skittish horses. Now follow me.'

Devlin wanted to ask about the river – where the water had gone; why it was dry – but every time he tried to speak, Siarl met him with either a taciturn silence or a grunt.

Sharp boulders jutted up through the hard dirt of a track snaking precariously down the side of the hill. The pack horse, still tethered to the stallion, slipped and slid under the weight of its load, and Devlin and Shay followed cautiously as Siarl navigated the path of razor-sharp rocks.

They stepped from the path into clumps of dry, prickly bushes and thick tufts of tall grasses. The banks were strewn with the huge, jagged trunks of trees.

'Over here,' Siarl growled. 'This is the spot indicated on the map. We will walk the horses across. Dismount now. I have no wish to cross in the dark. Hurry. I told you to hurry.'

As he spoke the rumble from the mountains

turned into a roar; the skies opened and a wall of water spilled down into the dry riverbed.

CHAPTER 5

S hay sat upright and rigid in the saddle. There was no way she was getting off her horse and into that river. Her eyes bore into her brothers' backs, silently willing them to acknowledge her presence. She pulled her hood tighter around her face as the bitter wind whipped up the gritty dirt of the hard plains.

They had ridden for three days, and another cold night loomed as they approached the River of Promise. Siarl led, as he had from the beginning, and never turned to check on his younger siblings. Devlin followed Siarl, keeping his own counsel, as Shay had trailed behind, conscious of her brother's simmering anger at her presence.

She was angry too. Not once had they asked her why she was there, what had made their mother send her with them. She thought of her mother, felt her hand on her shoulder, and heard the words again...

'It's time your lessons began,' Bedwynn said as her daughter sat huddled on the steps of the Keep, in the shadows of the clouds. She'd been watching Devlin follow Siarl and their uncle across the cobblestones to the training yard. 'Come with me to my chamber.' Shay followed her mother back into the Keep, up the narrow stairs and into the private bedchamber of her parents.

This had always been her favourite room: she loved clambering up the wooden steps onto the huge canopied bed, especially the creaking of the rope springs when she bounced on the feather-filled mattress. In the winter, a log fire roared in the large fireplace, the flames lighting up tapestries on the red granite walls.

Today should have been a warm summer's day, yet chilly breezes floated through the arched windows and she knelt on the padded window seat, looking out over the blue waters of the Bay of Rosemerta at the tattered sails of the ships moored along the quayside, the only colour left on the horizon.

A low red stone bench filled one corner of the chamber. In the four corners were a crimson candle, a silver bowl of water, a blue ceramic jar of earth and the multi-coloured feather of a painted bird – the four elements of the world: fire, water, earth and air. A small, carved wooden box with a tiny golden lock sat in the centre of the room, below a gilded mirror reflecting the blue waters of the bay. Large, colourful cushions lay scattered across the stone floor.

Shay scowled at her mother. The last thing she wanted to do was sit at the tapestry frame or pick up a calligraphy pen, not with all the activity in the courtyard below. It should have been her down there preparing for the journey – not Devlin. The prophecy hadn't said anything about a boy. But although she had argued with her uncle and Siarl, they had ignored her pleas. After all, she was a girl. She was dreading the coming days and weeks, trapped at the table in the Solar, practising her letters or her stitches while Devlin rode north to the army with Siarl. Bedwynn sunk into a cushion, and patted the one next to her. 'Come, Shay, sit with me a while. There are things you need to know.'

The further they rode, the more Devlin had thought about the old stories. There were images on the tapestries of green, fertile fields, but on their journey he now saw only fields of brown stubble. Before the Stones had been stolen, sheep and cattle had grazed on the pastures.

Crops had flourished, fed by the flowing waters of the River of Promise.

Two Seeding festivals had passed since the loss of the Stones. The storehouses were now almost empty. Without the Stones, the crops would shrivel in the ground again. The people would eventually starve.

Heavy clouds tossed spears of lightning down from the dark sky. The wind rose and the torrent of rain transformed the gravelly soil on the riverbank into a sea of mud.

Devlin felt the ground tremble. He leaned forward in the saddle and patted Cato as the horse pulled at the reins.

'It's all right,' he said, whispering into Cato's ear.

Shay felt a shiver run down her spine and she quickly ran her fingers over her necklace of smooth stones.

'Come on, Devlin,' she said as she passed him, edging Emilia towards the slippery bank. 'Siarl says this is where we can cross the river safely.

Are you ready?'

Cato whinnied at his stablemate, stomping a foreleg in the mud.

'Cato's ready,' Devlin said.

'Well, well, sister, anxious to cross?' Siarl said, pulling the copper visor down over his dark eyes.

'Be warned. The crossing will be dangerous. The rocks are rough and jagged, and now they will be slippery. But we need to be over by nightfall.'

He wrapped his cloak around his body.

'The wind is blowing hard, the rain heavier, and there is no shelter on this side. Hurry, if you want to sleep safely tonight.' He pointed across the river to a large oak, the thick trunk unyielding in the strengthening storm. The wide branches swayed and bent in defiance of the rising wind.

'We will camp beneath the oak.' As he spoke, a thunderous cracking filled the air, and the earth shuddered again.

Siarl led them right to the edge of the water, and the horses began to slide and lose their footing in the sticky mud.

'Make sure you follow directly behind me. Step your mounts into the footsteps of my horse,' Siarl said as he edged the huge warhorse down into the river.

Shay and Devlin followed and the water began to swirl around Cato and Emilia.

Shay leaned across to her brother and whispered, 'I know you are angry with me, Devlin, but believe me, you will need me before this journey ends.'

Devlin glared at her as he flicked the reins, encouraging Cato into the deeper water. The rain pounded down and the river rose higher.

Suddenly, his horse lost its footing on slippery rocks and Devlin slid from his saddle. He clung to Cato's thick mane as the torrents swirled furiously around his chest. Then his fingers slipped from the pommel and he was swallowed up by the raging water.

Shay screamed out to Siarl to stop, but he simply turned, lifted his visor and looked at them. With a smile on his thin lips, he kicked the flanks of his horse and pushed through the churning river to climb up the far bank.

Devlin frantically grabbed and grasped in the water. He didn't know what his fingers were searching for, he just knew he needed to find some way of fighting the force trying to carry him away.

Shay urged Emilia forward, her hooves slipping and sliding on the riverbed. She reached Devlin as he floundered between air and water. 'Grab hold!' she called above the noise of the storm.

Devlin grasped her hand and she pulled him close to Emilia's flank. He reached up and clutched at the reins while his horse, Cato, fought a strong current in the middle of the river.

Siarl, safely across the river, watched silently as his two siblings finally reached the bank and struggled to safety.

'Why didn't you help?' Devlin shouted, as he staggered and shivered through thick mud and sank down to the ground. His dark hair hung plastered across his pale face.

Siarl looked at them for a few moments before speaking. 'I could see you didn't need my help,' he said coldly. 'Shay said she could handle the journey. She needed to prove herself.'

'But we could have drowned,' said Devlin, still coughing up river water.

'Well, lucky you didn't,' Siarl said, with an ugly twist of his mouth. 'Now, help me set up camp. We can spend the night here. Tomorrow we head to the Sands of Sorrow, and from there into the foothills of the Tainted Mountains.' He led his horse to the tree and calmly pulled off the saddle as if nothing had happened.

Shay and Devlin stood trembling in their wet clothes as they watched him prepare the campsite. 'Don't just stand there,' Siarl called. 'Gather some wood if you want a fire. Makes no difference to me if you freeze in wet clothes, but I want to get warm.' He pulled off his sodden cloak and hung it from a branch of the tree.

"How can we find firewood when everything is so wet?" Devlin asked through chattering teeth.

"You have clearly not learnt enough for survival, little brother," Siarl retorted without looking at Devlin as he spoke.

'What's going on?' Devlin asked Shay. For the first time on their journey, his tone with her softened. 'We nearly died, and Siarl is acting as if nothing happened.'

'Let's collect the wood anyway,' Shay said. 'I don't know what's going on, but I'm cold and hungry. At least the pack horse made it across the river.' She pointed to the small horse emerging from bushes at the edge of the river. 'And all the supplies are still on him. But where's Cato?'

Devlin turned, expecting to see Cato already up the riverbank. He ran to the edge of the water, calling to his horse. 'Where is he? He can't have drowned – not Cato! He must be somewhere.' His voice was becoming desperate as he rushed along the bank. 'He must have swum to the other side. I'm going back to get him.'

Shay clutched his arm. 'He's gone, either back the way we came, or washed further down the river. If he was still near, you'd be able to see him.'

Devlin blinked back tears. 'No, you're wrong,' he said. 'We can't go on without Cato. He must be somewhere close by. He wouldn't leave me.' He dashed along the bank, darting in and out of rocks and bushes, calling for his horse.

'Stop that snivelling, boy,' Siarl snarled, casting a chilly shadow across Devlin, then slowly turning to Shay. 'The horse has gone,' he said to her. 'Devlin can share your mount.' As Shay started to protest, he added, 'If you don't like it, you can leave now – but your horse stays with us.'

'I don't care what you say, I want to cross back,' Devlin shouted over to Shay as he ran down to the river again. 'Cato's just wandered off. Maybe he's gone back to the village.'

Shay tethered Emilia to a small tree next to the river, making sure the knot was tight, then she went along the riverbank to where Devlin was now sitting with his back against the tree, his arms wrapped tightly round his knees.

'Help me collect some firewood,' she said quietly. 'You can't cross now – the river is getting deeper and deeper. Cato will come back. You know he would never leave you. He'll be back. Just wait and see. We can look for him in the morning.'

Devlin stood, sullenly kicking up dirt as he watched Shay gather armfuls of small broken branches. The wood was damp, so Siarl fed the fire with leaves and brown grass first, blowing on the embers as the flames slowly took hold.

Night fell rapidly. They huddled close to the fire, chewing on tough salted meat, washed down with water.

Finally, Siarl stood up and stretched his legs. He pulled his cloak from the tree branch. 'I'm going to sleep,' he said. 'You should do the same. Tomorrow will be a long day.' He settled on the edge of the campsite, pulling the cloak round his spindly body, and laid his head on his saddle.

Shay and Devlin unbuckled their sword belts, placed their shields on the ground and huddled together beneath Shay's cloak as the warmth from the fire comforted them until they slept.

CHAPTER
6

The wind howled like a banshee. In the middle of the night, the whinnying of horses and the stamping of hooves woke the children from a restless sleep. Funnels of dirt, stirred by the churning wind, whipped through the campsite.

'Devlin. Devlin, are you awake?' Shay shouted, shaking him awake. 'What's happening?

Devlin rose himself and scanned the campsite through the flying grains of dust and dirt.

'I can't see Siarl!' he cried. 'Where's Siarl?' Devlin leaped to his feet. He dashed to the far side of the oak tree, calling for his brother. The moon disappeared behind a bank of dark clouds.

'He's gone! Siarl has gone!' he called to Shay over the screeching wind.

She ran to his side, her cloak trailing through the swirling leaves.

'But he must be somewhere. He wouldn't abandon us,' Devlin said, his steadying his voice. 'Mother trusted him to take us to Father. Why would he leave?'

'He was angry because of me,' Shay said. 'He didn't want me to come but Mother made him.'

The wind dropped – and suddenly dark shapes swept down from the branches, snarling and snapping in the shadows before twisting above the dying embers of the fire. Bloodcurdling screams pierced the still night air as glowing orange eyes streaked around the campsite like fireflies.

They were being attacked!

The beasts multiplied. They were small but they were quick. They had thick, stubby arms and legs, covered in black scales, and razor-sharp horns.

Devlin and Shay stood with their backs pressed against each other as the beasts dived towards them, their sharp claws exposed in the moonlight. Then Devlin saw Shay reach for a necklace he had never noticed before and he felt a rush of sudden warmth flow through her body. The creatures pulled back, shrieking in pain as the flames from the last evening's fire leaped high into the night sky, lighting up the campsite.

'The flames!' Devlin roared out above the clamour. 'They're afraid of the flames.'

'Grab your sword,' Shay shouted, thrusting the hilt of a sword at him as she grabbed for her shield. 'And your shield. They're coming at us again.'

Devlin groped in the dark for his shield. Shay moved to his side, brandishing her sword above her head. From the corner of his eye, Devlin saw one of the beasts charge right at her. Its horn protruded above a single orange eye which illuminated up a misshapen scaly face with a flat skull.

He clutched his shield to his chest as he dragged a burning log from the fire and the beast flailed in fright at the flames. Devlin grasped the unburnt end of the log, raised it above his head and brandished it in wide circles, plunging into scales and glowing eyes as he tried to force their attackers into the fire.

Shay swung her sword down, cutting a bloody swathe through the shrieking creatures as they struggled to escape the flames. Once again, standing back to back, they fought for their lives as the hard work of the training yard proved its worth.

'Dip your sword into the flame!' Devlin cried above the clamour. He thrust his own sword into the flames, pulled it back and plunged the sword deep into the scales of the nearest creature.

A spray of steaming liquid burst out from the punctured scales and more bloodcurdling screams rose from the throats of the beasts. With each thrust, black scales tumbled like rocks of charred flesh into the sizzling flames.

'What are they? Where have they gone?' Shay gasped for breath as she collapsed onto the ground. Her curls, covered in ash, hung limp and damp across her face.

Devlin dropped his sword and fell down next to her. 'I don't know,' he said. 'They came down from the tree.' He lay on his back and looked up into the branches. 'They're gone now – for good, I hope.' He pulled himself up onto his elbow and looked thoughtfully at Shay. 'There was a mark on the map, like a black dot within a circle. I asked Siarl what it was. He said it marked a safe resting place. When we crossed the river and I saw the tree, I thought we'd be safe here.'

'Well, we weren't,' Shay said. 'Siarl was determined that we should cross the river. He didn't want to camp back on the other side. And now he's gone.'

'Maybe he's gone back to Rosemerta Castle, or one of the villages, to get help,' Devlin said, even though he didn't really believe his own words.

'You don't really think that's what's happened, do you?' she said. 'He's taken the pack horse, and probably Cato too. If he were coming back he would at least have left us with the supplies.'

'That means we haven't got any food,' Devlin said. 'We'll have to go back. The villagers will help us.'

'With what? They don't have enough to feed themselves,' Shay said, gripping her sword hilt until her knuckles hurt. 'I knew Siarl would betray us.'

'How?' Devlin let out a long sigh. 'Siarl is our brother. I'm sure he's gone to get help.' But Devlin replied as if he were answering his own question. 'Maybe we should wait here for him.'

Shay ignored her brother and continued.

'While you were preparing for the journey, I saw him sneak around behind the stables. I followed him. I thought he was alone, and then I heard him talking to someone in the shadows. I couldn't see who it was, but I heard what he said: "Master, I will carry out your orders. The boy will never return to Rosemerta." He turned and I just had time to duck around the corner. He didn't see me, but I know what I heard.'

Devlin was aghast. 'So he's a traitor,' he whispered, still barely able to believe Siarl would betray them. Then he tried to think about what to do again.

'The loss of the food doesn't matter anyway,' he said. 'We can't go on. We don't have the map. How will we find our way?'

'Think,' Shay replied. 'You saw it. Uncle Caedmon showed it to you in the Solar. Is there anything you can remember?'

'I'll try,' Devlin said, turning his mind back to the day he had studied the map.

'Uncle Caedmon spread it out on the table.

He pointed out the dangers, like sinkholes in the desert. And he warned me about the Tywyll; the dark forest of the Tainted Mountains. Uncle said we have to stay on a particular path when we reach the mountains, and only travel in daylight. Siarl said that would take too long and suggested a different route – through the Tywyll – but Uncle said that path was dangerous. I can't remember everything, but I think I can probably mark out the trail Uncle showed us.'

'Well, at least we know we shouldn't trust anything Siarl told us,' Shay said. 'Maybe he was the one who drew the map. We'll just have to keep a watch for danger. After all, we just beat the tree creatures, so we can do anything now.' She sounded very sure of herself. 'We should follow that trail to the mountains then,' she said firmly.

Devlin looked at his sister, wishing he had the same level of confidence. He picked up a stick and began to draw shapes in the dirt.

'We are here, on this side of the river,' he said,

pointing the stick at the roughly drawn lines. 'To continue, we will have to cross the desert just to the north of the river. We're almost there already. Then we will reach the Tainted Mountains.' He pointed at the horizon. 'When the sun comes up we'll be able to see the mountains in the distance. The sun is rising on our left, so that's the east. It will cross the sky to the west, so north is where I'm pointing to. The map had a cross like this' – he marked an x in the dust – 'and the word sentinel. I asked Uncle Caedmon what it was. All he said was that it was a pointer for our journey and Siarl would explain when we got there.'

'Well, Siarl's gone, and we're not turning back.' Shay stood in front of him with her arms crossed determinedly over her chest.

'But we still haven't got any food and it would be madness to go into the desert without water,' Devlin replied.

'Lucky for us that before I left I sneaked into the kitchens and filled a sack with dry biscuits and smoked meat,' said Shay. 'I have a big leather bottle for our water too. Let's fill it from the river. We'll have to be careful with our remaining food, but once we're over the Sands of Sorrow we can find fruit and berries.'

Devlin listened, amazed at Shay's resourcefulness. Not that he would ever admit it to her, of course.

'Once we start to cross the desert we can rest,' he said, feeling a bit more confident now. He pointed his stick at circles drawn on wiggly lines showing sand dunes. 'These are waterholes.'

'What is this?' Shay said. She knelt down and her fingers traced along a straight line with a circle on top.

'You've put it halfway between the river and the foothills of the mountains.'

'I can't remember. I just know it was there,' Devlin answered. 'It had a word next to it. Oasis, or something like that. Uncle Caedmon just said Siarl would make sure we got through the desert. Maybe we should go round it. We can'y trust Siarl any more. He knew what was out here and he abandoned us. Maybe that's why...'

He paused, thinking. 'He was afraid. After all, he had to pass through this way to get home.'

'No, that's not why he's gone,' Shay said. 'Although I'm sure he knew about the creatures at the river. That's why he left. I'm sure he expected us to die at the river. He wouldn't think we'd ever try to make it over the desert and into the Tainted Mountains.' She stood up and skipped around Devlin, laughing as she spoke.

'Well, that wasn't very clever of him, was it? We have already crossed the River of Promise and he probably thought those scaly beasts would tear us apart. Well, they didn't. We were too clever for them. If there's anything else out there we can beat it.'

Devlin looked at her and suddenly he knew they could do this. They must complete the task entrusted to them. They were children of Lord

Padraig of Rosemerta. They must continue their journey and free the army from the clutches of the Dark Lord.

'We'd better get going then,' he said.

Shay looked around the campsite, at their belongings scattered across the ground.

'Emilia,' she called out in surprise as the white horse trotted to her side, the loose reins dragging behind.

CHAPTER
7

'Maybe I should cross back over first? Cato might be in the village. It's not very far,' Devlin said. He stared hopefully back across the river.

'We haven't got time,' Shay said. 'Cato's probably halfway back to the castle by now. At least we still have Emilia. Lucky I tethered her away from the tree.'

'That's why I don't think Siarl's got Cato,' Devlin said. 'He would have taken Emilia as well. If he wants us to die out here, he'd have taken not only all our supplies but also both horses.'

Shay snorted. 'Well, he couldn't have taken Emilia. I'd tethered her to a tree, but she would have woken me if anyone had tried to take her. She wouldn't have let him near her. Help me saddle her up. We're going now – unless you want to spend another night here?'

Devlin looked at her and then back over the river to where they had come from. Then he reluctantly pulled himself up into the saddle and rode behind Shay, still thinking about Cato, lost on the Plains of Rosemerta.

'If Cato goes home without me, Mother will think something has happened to us,' he said. 'She'll send someone out to look for us.'

'Who? There's no one left,' Shay said. 'Uncle Caedmon and some boys from the kitchen? I don't think so. They'll just think Cato's run off and we're still following the map. After all, Emilia won't be with Cato.'

Devlin didn't look convinced, but the scowl on his face told Shay to change the subject before Devlin had a chance to reply. 'Can you see the dragon in the mountains?'

They had grown up listening to Uncle Caedmon's tales of a black dragon swooping down from hidden eyries and attacking unsuspecting travellers.

'That's just the wind blowing the dark storm clouds through the mountains,' Devlin replied. 'They'll be gone before we reach them.'

He sighed. 'We have a long way to go. First, we have to cross the Sands of Sorrow.

Shay urged the horse over the rough path and they rode on for several hours. The cool morning breeze heated up as the sun rose in the sky and Emilia's hooves began to sink into sand, hard and low at first, before rolling sand dunes emerged, growing higher the further they travelled.

Emilia struggled with each step now as she climbed the dunes. It was becoming hotter and hotter, the sand softer and softer, and the children took frequent sips from the bottle of water, aware that the flask would soon be empty.

'Look, Devlin, down there! Can you see some trees?' Shay said suddenly, shielding her eyes from the sun with her hand. 'Shade! Let's stop there. It's too hot to continue now and Emilia needs a rest. Maybe it's a waterhole.'

'Perhaps it's the oasis marked on Siarl's map. It might not be safe,' Devlin said.

'We'll have to take that chance,' Shay replied. 'Emilia needs water too. We should stay there now until dark, I think, then get moving again while it's cool. There are no clouds and the moon is waxing, so we should have plenty of light tonight.'

Emilia pulled back her ears, snorted, and stepped forward, heading further into the Sands of Sorrow as the sun rose higher in the sky. It was further than it looked to get to the shade, past clumps of dead trees and empty waterholes.

At the base of the next dune, Devlin slid from

the saddle and led their tired horse up through the grainy sand.

'We're nearly there,' Shay said as they reached the high point of the dune. She pointed to a cluster of palm trees nestling around the edge of a crystal-clear lagoon of water.

The pool was shimmering in the sun. A wall of yellow dunes surrounded the oasis. In fact, from their vantage point, the desert rolled on for ever, like rippling waves on a dead sea. They could just make out the peaks of the mountains rising above a purple heat haze floating on the horizon.

'See,' Shay said. 'The dragon's breath is on the mountains. Just like the tapestry – the one in the Great Hall above the fireplace.'

'It's not the dragon's breath,' Devlin said. 'There's no such thing. They're just stories to scare little children into being good. Are you scared?'

He sensed her reaction to the taunt before she turned. As Shay threw herself at him from her saddle he stepped aside and she fell into the sand.

'Not as quick as you thought,' he said, but Shay kicked out with one leg and Devlin dropped. His mouth filled with sand, but they wrestled in the soft sand until Devlin pulled back.

'What are we doing?' he said. 'We're alone in a desert and we're fighting when we should be helping each other.' He stood up and held his hand out to Shay.

They stood side by side as the sun stretched to the highest point in the sky. Finally reaching the shade of the trees, they unsaddled the horse and refilled their empty water bottle. Emilia gratefully dipped her long white muzzle into the cool water.

'Let's rest here until sunset.' Shay lay her cloak on the grass.

'What about the sinkholes if we travel in the dark?' Devlin asked. 'Uncle showed me the circles marking them on the map and told me to beware of hidden danger. Siarl laughed and said they were nothing. "You're frightening the boy, old man," he said. "There are no dangers in the desert apart from the sun." I think we need to cross the Sands as quickly as we can,' he added. 'Find fresh water and pasture for Emilia. We can replenish our supplies further on.'

'We can't trust anything Siarl said,' Shay said. 'But I think we should stay here until dark. It's too hot to go any further anyway, and Emilia needs the rest. Let's eat something.'

She pointed at the ground. 'Look – there are dates and apricots lying here. We can even take some with us. If the map brought us to the oasis then there must be other safe places ahead.'

As they gorged on the fruit, Devlin leaned back against a tree and looked at Shay. 'You haven't yet told me why Mother sent you,' he said.

'That's because you never asked.' Shay pulled a necklace of polished beads from beneath her tunic and ran her fingers across their surface.

'I was angry when you appeared at the gates,' Devlin said. 'Nothing had been said. It wasn't fair. I hadn't seen you for days, and then suddenly you're coming with us. Why? Did you badger Mother until she gave in?'

Shay sighed. 'It wasn't like that. Yes, I was angry that everyone assumed that the message was meant for you. I was sitting on the steps of the Keep watching you and Siarl. Mother came to get me.'

She looked into the distance and remembered.

The fragrant odour of incense filled the chamber and candles burned on the granite bench. Bedwynn opened a purse hanging at her waist and pulled out a small golden key. She placed the key in the lock of the carved box in the centre of the room, opened it and lifted out a necklace of four polished stones.

'For you,' she said, draping the stones around Shay's neck.

'What are they?' the girl said as she looked

in the mirror above the bench. She ran her fingers across each one: turquoise blue, warm amber, jet black and fiery red.

'They are the Stones of Aarush. My mother gave them to me when I left my home, and now I am passing them to you,' Bedwynn said.

'They're beautiful, but I'm not going anywhere,' Shay replied.

'I am sending you with your brothers.'

Shay felt her heart leap, whether in fear or joy she wasn't sure.

'Yes,' her mother continued. 'But first I must teach you many things: the way of the Stones, and how to read the power of the elements that surround us. You and I are daughters of Aarush. It is time you learned of your heritage.'

As her mother continued to speak, Shay listened carefully, her eyes widening. She felt excited by what she heard, but mostly she focused on her mother's final words: 'Devlin and Siarl will need you.'

'I can't wait to tell Devlin,' she said, then

laughed. 'He won't be happy.'

'No, not yet,' her mother said. 'Your uncle will try to stop you. I will talk to him first. Siarl... he is unhappy, but he refuses to talk to me. I think he is worried enough about taking Devlin with him. He is the only one who knows what lies beyond the plains and the river. No, it's best if we don't say anything just yet. We still have several days before you leave and I have much to teach you in this time.'

She spoke true. Shay barely saw her brothers until the day arrived when they would leave the castle. As they were loading up the pack horse, Bedwynn called Shay to her side.

'It's time,' she said. 'Your horse is ready. Your brothers are at the gate. I have just been speaking to Devlin. Ride . . . and remember: they will need you.'

'I'm glad you are here,' Devlin said when Shay had finished her story. 'Siarl meant to leave me alone to die. He probably thought you were weak and would slow us down. He was pretending to be angry that you came.'

'No, I think he suspected something,' Shay replied. 'He knows about the Aarush and their powers. We all knew where Mother came from. He knew more than we did, that's why he was angry with her.'

'It was you who saved us at the river,' Devlin said.

Shay looked at him and smiled. 'We need to rest. We've got a long way to go.'

Emilia nuzzled Shay. She stretched out and shook Devlin awake. 'It's time to go,' she said, looking up at the curtain of stars sparkling against the ink-black sky. A full moon threw its yellow light across the oasis.

Together they saddled the horse, refilled their water bottle and collected fruit to fill the saddlebags. Then they began the hard climb up the nearest sand dune.

'What if clouds cover the moon? How do

we find north?' Shay wondered. 'I know how to find north with the passage of the sun, but at night . . .'

'Easy,' said Devlin. 'The moon was on the horizon before we fell asleep. When the moon rises before sunset, the bright side is west. Even with clouds, we'll still get some moonlight. So we go this way.' She pointed across the moonlit sand to the white peaks of the mountains, shining like beacons against the black sky.

'Is that something Uncle taught you?'

He looked at her and grinned. 'Yes, and now you know it too.'

They looked back on the oasis. In the moonlight, the water glistened and the palms swayed in the breeze. The rippling desert stretched out for miles. Lizards and snakes scuttled across the white sand.

They rode for what seemed like hours. A cool breeze blew across the desert. They stopped only to share their water with Emilia, or to nibble on dates.

Orange rays of the morning light rose on the horizon. 'It will be dawn soon,' Devlin said, looking up at the moon as it tracked across the night sky. 'The map showed another oasis. We can stop there. Tomorrow we should be in the foothills of the mountains.'

But they were not safe yet.

Hot blasts of wind suddenly whipped in a frenzy, tossing dirt and grit into the air, and a long wall of swirling sand covered the desert like a black fog. Thunder cracked as the sand rose up, blinding them. The Tainted Mountains were lost to sight as the sandstorm whirled around them.

'Devlin, Devlin,' Shay called out above the roar of wind and sand. 'We have to stop.'

Devlin, barely able to hear anything above the screeching wind, knew she was right.

Shay pulled Emilia up and they dismounted. 'Quick, wrap your scarf around your mouth,' she shouted in the darkness.

'Down, get down,' she called to Devlin.

Emilia dropped to the ground and wrapped her body around them as the sandstorm blasted overhead. They scrambled in the sand, digging out a hollow with their bare hands. Huddled together in the trough of sand, pulling the cloaks over their heads, and over Emilia's nostrils, they clung to each other as the storm swept over them.

Just as suddenly as the wind had blown up, it stopped. An eerie silence filled the air as Devlin and Shay struggled to climb out of the hollow and Emilia scrambled to her feet, throwing off the heavy layer of sand covering her body.

Devlin and Shay pulled back their cloaks and crawled out, then stood up and looked around. The landscape had changed. Ripples of sand had turned into high dunes, dunes into flat desert land. The sun was rising in the sky and the heat was becoming dry and oppressive.

Devlin looked at Shay and started to laugh.

'What's so funny?' she said. 'We could have

died in a sandstorm and you're laughing.'

'It's your face,' he said, laughing and spinning in the sand. It's muddy, like streaks of red mud running down your face.'

'Yours is no better,' Shay retorted. 'It looks like you're crying, only the tears are red.'

Devlin lifted his hand, ran his fingers down his cheek and felt a layer of gritty dirt on his face. 'My eyes were watering. The sand must have come through the cloak,' he said. 'At least we're not dead.'

As he spoke, he saw a movement behind him and he turned to see the horse trot across the sand.

'Emilia, Emilia, come back,' Devlin called. He chased the wandering horse to the base of a steep sand dune, but Shay passed him and began to climb the crest of the dune.

'The mountains, I can see the mountains,' she said, facing the mountain range.

A narrow strip of red stones led from the desert to the low hills huddled in the shadow of the mountains. Snow covered the highest peaks, shimmering in the sunlight and Devlin lifted his hand to shade his eyes from the glare.

The gleam of snow outlined a black marker towering above a dark canopy of trees. 'Just below the snowline,' he said, pointing. 'That must be the sentinel, in the forest, in the Tywyll. Uncle said the sentinel was in the forest. But look at the cliffs. They really do look like dragons. They're covered in dragon's scales, and the ridges look like the sharp teeth of the dragon in the drawings.'

'If we hurry we can make camp at the base of the Tainted Mountains,' Shay said. 'We shouldn't enter the Tywyll after dark.'

'And why would that be?' Devlin asked, throwing his sister a look of confidence.

CHAPTER
8

S hay flicked the reins, and gently encouraged the horse to step carefully over the layer of polished red stones. They spread out like a patterned pavement between the desert and the hills.

'We're nearly there,' she said as the path narrowed and stunted, thorny bushes slowly gave way to groves of trees. They'd been travelling for several hours and she was glad to see the trees.

'We can camp beneath the trees,' Devlin said. 'The day is only half over,' Shay replied. 'Shouldn't we keep moving? At least try and get beyond the foothills by tonight.'

'I'm tired,' he moaned. 'We've been travelling for six days now. We were up all last night, we've just crossed a desert and we're exhausted. Look at the trees. They're full of walnuts. And listen, that sounds like a creek. We've used up nearly all our water. There's plenty of grass for Emilia. No, we should stop for the rest of the day, and stay here for the night too.'

Shay, still exhausted from the heat of the desert and too tired to argue, hated to admit Devlin was right. Her horse bent down and began to nibble on the grass. It was lush and green. 'All right,' she said, 'but only because of Emilia. I still think we should go further.'

Devlin smiled to himself. *How typical*, he thought. Shay always had to have the last word, but at least this time she agreed with him.

After heaving the saddle and bags from the horse, Shay led Emilia to the creek. They drank until their stomachs filled with the cool water, then lay in the shade of a tree. Just as Shay drifted off to sleep she heard Devlin jump up and climb the thick trunk of the tree.

'What are you doing?' she called.

'Picking walnuts. Here, catch.'

She ducked as he threw a handful of nuts at her.

'We can fill one of the bags,' he said.

Shay gathered the nuts and sat down on the grass. She pulled out her dagger and, using the hilt, began to crack open the hard shells.

'Throw down some more, these are delicious.'

When Devlin climbed down, a pile of shelled walnuts waited for him.

The rest of the day and the night passed uneventfully.

They woke to bright rays of sun filtering through the trees, warming their bodies. As they breakfasted on berries and more walnuts, Devlin thought how wrong he had been to want Shay to stay at home. They were a team.

After the river and the desert, he was certain they could finish the journey, but finding and rescuing the lost army, he wasn't so sure. He pictured the map in his mind. The path would lead them beyond the Tainted Mountains, into the Frozen Northlands to face unknown perils.

The sun climbed in the sky as they set off. The breeze chilled as it drifted across the rocky twisting path and they began the climb into the hills. Sometime in the afternoon, they paused at the top of the last hill and looked forward over a forest covering the lower reaches of the mountains.

They had reached the Tywyll.

Their sure-footed white horse continued to pick her way along the stony trail. Thick tangled roots from towering trees crossed the path, blocking out the light, and large boulders clung to rocky ledges, overshadowing the narrow pass. The wind stilled as twilight neared. And as they climbed further, the sun disappeared behind a bank of black clouds, and the first signs of night appeared in silver slivers of light from a rising moon, breaking through the dense canopy.

'We should make camp before we lose the light,' Shay said. The horse reared and strained on the reins.

'There is danger in the air. I think Emilia senses it. If we encounter anything we'll be defenceless in the dark.'

'Let's look for a good spot then,' Devlin agreed. He looked around nervously. The trees appeared to cast flitting shadows all about them.

'Devlin, Devlin,' whispered Shay. 'There is something up ahead. I just saw shadows dart across the path.'

He stared long hard in the direction Shay pointed but could see nothing.

'It must be your imagination,' he said, willing his words to be true. 'After everything that's happened your mind is playing tricks.'

'There is something in the trees,' Shay replied,

annoyed that Devlin seemed to be dismissing her fears. Emilia's ears pricked up. She stomped into the ground, forcing Shay to pull hard on the reins.

'Then we won't camp here tonight,' said Devlin, thinking this was better than admitting he shared her fears. 'We'll go a little further. We should be safe further in.'

'There it is!' cried Shay as she pointed into the trees encroaching onto the path ahead. 'Something's up there!'

Devlin peered into the darkness. The wind rose again and a dark shape hissed, spitting out globs of black slime as it soared above them. Huge flailing wings broke down branches, blocking the path.

'Look out!' he called as he felt a stream of slime slide down his arm. He gripped Shay as she struggled to control the rearing horse. 'It's coming straight at us. Duck, quickly!'

He watched, transfixed, at the sight of the black monster swooping and diving between the trees. He felt sure he had seen it somewhere before, but fear blocked his memory. Bulbous eyes protruded from either side of a small skull. Spiked fangs jutted out like daggers from a blood-red mouth as talons clawed and slashed through the air.

Emilia reared up, thrashing her hooves at the creature. She twisted and turned, desperate to dodge the attack as she raced up the path. Then, just as the talons reached for them, the creature flew screeching back above the trees. The horse galloped up the path, weaving nimbly past broken branches and fallen boulders.

A bloodcurdling scream filled the air. The creature plunged back down through the trees, straining its rippling wings, trying to force them from the path and over into a steep ravine. Lifting its feathered body, the creature flew back up into the trees, circling its fleeing prey.

Shay pulled hard on the reins in a desperate race to escape the talons hurtling towards them. They turned a sharp bend and the trees disappeared behind a wall of mist. They plunged through. A flash of light almost blinded them as Emilia halted in the middle of a clearing. The creature dived at them repeatedly but each time pulled back, shrieking wildly as if it had hit an invisible wall.

'We made it.' Shay leaned forward, hugging her horse, who was breathing heavily. 'The sentinel!'

A tall black marker stone pointed toward the skies. A sudden flash of light illuminated rows of drawings and symbols etched into the surface of the stone.

'What just happened? What was that light?' How will we get out?' Devlin said as they dismounted. He scanned the clearing as they approached the stone pillar. 'Look at those markings, the circles and the drawings. We've seen them before.' Something about the sentinel nagged at him.

'We know the map had circles at the river. Were there any more circles on the map? Anything around the sentinel?' Shay asked.

'What can you remember?'

'The Tywyll was marked, but I don't remember any circles in the forest. Nothing until the Ice Citadel.' Then Devlin stopped and pointed at the stone marker.

'What?' Shay turned.

A light flickered behind the sentinel, highlighting strange circular patterns carved deep into its black stone... and a small old man scuttled out into the moonlight. His skin was brown and wrinkled, like the bark of a tree. Two thick plaits of faded green hair fell across a cloak made of leaves. He held a wooden staff in his calloused hand.

'Who are you?' they chorused.

His green eyes twinkled. His voice was soft and calm. 'Wealdrun of the Culchans, Keeper of the Tywyll.'

'Do you live in the forest?' Devlin asked.

'My people have always lived in the forest.'

'I didn't think you really existed! You're real,' Shay said as she bounced from foot to foot.

'I thought the Culchans only existed in our uncle's stories.'

'And how is my old friend Caedmon? It's been a long time since we last met. Now, that's enough from me. Why are two children and a horse travelling alone through the Tywyll? There are many dangers in the forest.'

'How do you know our uncle?' Devlin said, trying hard not to stare at the old man. He was short, almost the same height as Shay, with the same eyes – almost jade-green.

'Your Uncle amd I were friends a long time ago. Too many years to remember,' he said sadly, almost whispering. 'But you are safe now. The Brendts are gone. They are afraid of the marker. They know what it is.'

Devlin was still puzzled. How did the Weadrum know that Caedmon was *their* uncle? And even if the old man was telling the truth and they were safe now, what would happen when they left the clearing?

'What are Brendts? Where have they gone?'

Devlin scrambled for the words.

'Brendts are half-bat, half-raven. At night, they perch high in the canopy of the forest. When the sun rises, they retreat deep in the mountains, filling their lairs with the bleached bones of lost travellers.'

Wealdrun stared quietly out into the trees. His cloak of leaves rustled at the slightest movement. Then he spoke again.

'You haven't answered my question. Why are you here? What brings you to the sentinel?'

Shay stepped forward. 'We are headed to the Frozen Northlands of the Dark Lord,' she said. 'Drepe swept down on our country, the land of Rosemerta, two seedtimes past, and stole the Luchair Stones.'

She paused, feeling she needed to explain more, yet somehow knowing that the man in front of her knew this already.

'The Stones have protected us and kept the crops safe since the time of Isern, the Blacksmith King of the Raedlands. Lord Padraig, our father, led the Red army across the plains and into the mountains in pursuit of the Dark Lord. Since then we have heard nothing of their fate until Siarl, our brother, returned less than three weeks ago. He carried a message about a prophecy, and a map and—'

Devlin interrupted. 'News. Our father and the army are captives of the Dark Lord. But Siarl abandoned us at the River of Promise and horrible scaly creatures attacked us. We called out to our brother, but he had gone. And he took my horse.'

'That was four days ago,' Shay continued.

'Since then we've been travelling on our own. Siarl was supposed to lead us to the Ice Citadel. Now we need to find the Stones on our own and release the army and return home before the next seedtime or the crops will fail again. The grain stores are almost empty. The people will starve. We have to win back the Luchair Stones.'

'You have been handed a huge task,' Wealdrun

replied. 'Your Red army rode through the Tywyll. My people aided them, leading them through the mountain pass, up to the snowline and into the valley leading to the frozen lake and the Ice Citadel.'

'And then?' Devlin was anxious to hear more. 'Did the army find the Dark Lord?'

'It did, indeed,' Wealdrun confirmed. 'The two great armies confronted each other across the valley. Then from the safety of the trees, we watched as a knight from your Red army rode out, crossing over to the Dark army. Your father called out, cursing the knight for his treachery, and then the battle began. It was short but ferocious. Both armies drew their weapons and charged, and the valley thundered with the clashing of iron and cries of the dying and wounded.'

Shay put her hands to her face, horrified at the images the Culchan's words conjured up.

'A band of Brendts flew down as the lake rose,' Wealdrun concluded. 'The high waves turned into a thick wall of ice and entombed the army.'

'Our brother Siarl returned to Rosemerta with news of the battle,' Devlin said, 'and he told us about the army, frozen into the great glacier, but he didn't tell us how it happened. He said that as the battle was clearly lost, Father gave him the map and message about the prophecy, and told him to return to Rosemerta.' He paused and added angrily, 'Uncle Caedmon and our mother believed everything he said. But why would Siarl choose to betray us all?'

'Tell me about the message. I would like to hear more of this prophecy,' Wealdrun said. 'But first, follow me. I will take you to the village of the Culchans. You can rest and replenish your stores.'

'We don't have time,' Shay said. 'We have to keep going.'

The old man looked at them and his green eyes reflected the colours of the forest. Then he simply held out his hand.

Devlin grasped the outstretched fingers, and then turned to Shay. 'We have time,' he said to her softly.

'Follow me.' Wealdrun whispered the words as he led them to the other side of the sentinel where a blanket of brown leaves covered the ground. The old man lifted his staff, the leaves parted and an entrance into the earth opened up.

CHAPTER
9

Wealdrun sensed their unease. 'Come. Put away your fears,' the old man said as he stepped into the tunnel. He turned briefly to touch Emilia on the muzzle, as if he were communicating the same message to the horse. 'Wealdrun is right. We must follow him.'

Devlin turned and scanned the clearing. It was Shay's voice, but her lips had never moved. His eyes narrowed as he stared at Shay. Her green eyes smiled as she stroked the amber stone on her necklace.

'What?' he said. 'How did you do that?'

With Emilia's leather reins wrapped around one hand, Shay grasped Devlin's with the other, and together they stepped into the opening where Wealdrun waited patiently.

He held a burning torch aloft, the flickering flame lighting up the tunnel. Smiling gently he turned and led them into the darkness. They followed silently, still holding hands.

The tunnel twisted and spiralled down into the inner recesses of the earth. Tree roots pushed through the walls, threatening to trip them at every turn. Devlin touched the slimy lichen-covered walls. It was cold and damp to his touch and he shivered, pulling his cloak around his body and drawing the hood across his face.

The path narrowed as they hurried to keep up with Wealdrun, and for one short moment they were alone in the pitch dark of the tunnel. Using the wall to guide them, they turned a sharp corner and stepped into light.

Wealdrun stood in the middle of a wide, low-roofed cavern.

Devlin nudged Shay and whispered, 'The walls are the same colour as the castle,'

Her eyes widened with surprise at the sight of the pale red granite illuminated by the flames of the torch. Stepping closer she could see rough-hewn marks covering the walls, and she ran her fingers gently over them.

Wealdrun moved to her side and placed his arm round her shoulder.

'A long time ago this was part of the great quarry of the Raedlands, supplying building materials to the kingdom,' he said. 'One long, cold winter in the distant past, a Dark Lord led his legion of undead through the Tywyll. They thundered across the land on horses raised in the pits of the Underworld. The ground beneath their hooves shuddered. The quarry collapsed. My ancestors dug the tunnel in a desperate attempt to find survivors. There were none. This is all that remains.'

'But why?' asked Devlin. 'Where were they going?'

'This was in the time before the great upheaval that separated Aarush from the mainland. Every Dark Lord has made it his mission to control the Raedlands. Drepe has achieved what no other Dark Lord has done. As long as he holds the Luchair Stones, his power grows stronger, and the might of Rosemerta wanes. Soon he will turn his sights on Eraba and Aarush. But, enough. You will learn more when we reach Dalavich. We are only halfway there.'

He pulled the cloak of leaves around his body, lifted the torch and hurried across the cavern into another tunnel. The path rose and they saw ahead of them an arched wooden door. Wealdrun pulled a large black key from his belt and placed it in a brass lock. The door swung open and Devlin shielded his eyes against the bright sunlight that filled the tunnel.

Emilia pulled back and whinnied and Wealdrun

laid his hand once more on her neck and caressed her grey muzzle. The horse calmed again, nuzzling against the old man as he led them out into a clearing.

Small brown-skinned men, women and children, all like Wealdrun, surrounded them. The youngest of the children hid, shyly peeking out between the legs of their parents, their vivid green hair shining in the sun, distinct from the fading shades of the adults.

'These are my people,' Wealdrun said. 'We welcome you to Dalavich.'

The crowd parted and Wealdrun led them to a large oak tree surrounded by a timber building with a thatched roof. Smoke spiralled from a large campfire, and the smell of freshly baked bread filled the air.

They looked around. High cliffs surrounded the village and thick groves of trees clung to the rim. A ring of small huts encircled the tree, and a stream meandered through the clearing.

Wealdrun stepped up onto the wide porch of

the tree house. Devlin and Shay, surrounded by chattering Culchans, looked up at the old man. He opened his arms wide and spoke.

'I bring you children of Lord Padraig of Rosemerta.' His voice, strong and clear, echoed through the village. The Culchans edged closer to the porch. 'Devlin and Shay of Rosemerta seek shelter in Dalavich before they enter the Frozen Northlands.'

A gasp rose from the crowd and they whispered amongst themselves, glancing cautiously at the two children as they stood there, their heads high, their eyes full of resolve.

Shay nudged Devlin. 'They look like smaller, younger versions of Wealdrun.'

He nodded in return. *Maybe he's just got a big family*, he thought.

'No, Devlin, they're not my children.'

He jumped when he heard the words. Wealdrun had not spoken out loud. The words were in his head.

'We are a tribe, like the people of Rosemerta.

We are one.'

That night, sitting around the campfire, wrapped in blankets of woven flax, Shay and Devlin listened to the old people weave their stories of the past. Later, lying side by side in a wide hammock strung between two stout trees, they recounted the tales. For there were parts of the stories they had never before heard; had never been told by Caedmon.

'So Drepe is descended from Isern, just like us,' Shay said.

'And from the House of Rosemerta,' Devlin replied. 'Why weren't we told? I never read about it in the histories, and Uncle Caedmon never told us any stories about that time.' He paused. 'So, have I got it right? Edana, Drepe's ancestor, was the twin of Villeam, and they were the children of Luchair, first Lord of Rosemerta and eldest child of Isern. Edana was the first-born, and she turned the Frozen Northlands into a kingdom of evil, plotting and planning for the day when one of her descendants would grow strong enough to reclaim the Raedlands in her name.'

'She thought the kingdom should be hers,' Shay added. 'But the Culchans have been here a long time, Wealdrun said. They have seen the shadows of the Dark army sweeping across the cliff tops over the years, as generations of Dark Lords gathered the souls of executed criminals for his army of the undead, and kidnapped poor farming folk to serve him, taking on Edana's desire to conquer the Raedlands. Now Drepe has the Luchair Stones and his power grows stronger every day.' Shay shuddered as she finished, imagining a Rosemerta ruled by Drepe.

'We no longer have any choice,' Devlin said. 'We have to fight this evil. We have to continue.'

That night their dreams turned to nightmares. Images of starving people, toiling under the wrathful watch of Drepe's minions, disturbed their sleep. When morning arrived, they woke to the chatter of Culchans preparing food around the campfire.

'Good morning.'

They sat up. Wealdrun was standing next to the hammock.

'Just in time for the morning feast,' he said, and then he looked at Shay. 'After you eat, we need to speak. Devlin can spend some time learning the ways of my people.'

They climbed from the hammock. 'What's that about?' Devlin said. 'Why does Wealdrun want to speak to you and not me?'

'He probably wants to try and send me back. Well, it won't work,' Shay said, shrugging her shoulders.

Later, after they had eaten, Wealdrun beckoned Shay to his side. 'Come with me,' he said.

She followed him, through the village to the edge of the stream, where Wealdrun sat down in the shade of willow while Shay stood and watched the overhanging branches drift on the water. The sky was as clear and blue as the stream. She waited patiently for the old man to speak.

Finally he lifted his gaze from the stream and looked at her.

'Tell me about the string of beads,' he said.

'These?' Shay replied, with a nervous shake of her head. 'My mother gave them to me when I left Rosemerta.'

'I know,' he answered. 'I gave them to your mother a long time ago.'

Shay looked at him. Her mind raced in confusion. What was the old man talking about?

'How do you know my mother?' she whispered uncertainly.

The story slowly unravelled. She knew her mother was from the Isle of the Aarush, and – like her father – also descended from Isern the Blacksmith King. Aarush, Rosemerta and Eraba: the three lands of the Kingdom of the Raedlands.

'Are the Frozen Northlands part of the Raedlands then?' Shay said. 'After all, Drepe is a descendant of Isern too.'

Wealdrun smiled. 'No, that can never be. The Dark Lords have lost their souls. There is no goodness left in them, so they can never be part of the Raedlands.' He patted the ground and gestured for the girl to sit at his side. 'You are Aarush, like your mother. Like my people. We are the people left behind when the Aarush separated from the main island. Since then, Aarush and Culchan have crossed the waters, sharing our knowledge. Now it is time for you to learn.'

He took Shay over to the stream where he showed her how to use the beads to unlock the powers hidden deep in her mind.

'The turquoise is the stone of the skies,' he said. 'It will clear your mind and tell you what to do. Listen to the stone and you will stay safe.'

The black stone of obsidian, the blue of the turquoise, the golden glow of amber and the bright red ruby: each of the four stones held their own secrets and powers.

The lessons continued for six days.

Wealdrun even passed to Shay deep knowledge of the elements – earth, wind, air and fire – beyond her mother's lessons. He taught her the ways of the earth and its bounty. She learned how to use the plants of the forest, and how to brew special teas: teas to heal, and even teas to give them courage when needed most. He filled her pouch with herbs grown in the gardens of the village.

At first Shay kept her lessons secret from Devlin, worried that he would be angry to learn about her heritage. But each night he pestered her for information. When she finally told him, she was surprised at his reaction.

'I'm glad you came,' he said as they lay in the hammock. 'I don't feel so alone knowing that you are with me; knowing you have these skills. Maybe you are the Chosen One. You know so much now. It makes me feel safe.' He turned to his side.

Shay was soon fast asleep.

Meanwhile, Devlin was settling into life with the Culchans. The young men showed him the Culchan ways of fighting. He learned to thrust and defend with the short sword used by the men, and the trees became his friends as he studied the skills to survive in the forests.

One evening, as Wealdrun returned to the village with Shay, he said to her, 'We will have a feast tonight. It is time for the two of you to continue your journey. At first light I will lead you from the village.'

Shay nodded, and turned to fill her saddlebags. But Wealdrun stopped her.

'No,' he said. 'Your horse must stay behind. The north is no place for a horse.'

Shay protested. 'Drepe has horses. I've seen them. The army took their horses with them. Why can't I take my horse? We've never been parted before.'

'The horse will give you away. Do you want the Brendts to fly down again? No, you must travel on foot to the citadel.' He held up his hand to silence her as she tried to argue. 'If you cannot part from the horse then Devlin must go alone.'

'You know Devlin needs me.' She stamped her foot and turned angrily, placing her arms around Emilia's neck. A tear rolled down her cheek. 'I won't be long,' she whispered. 'You'll be safe here. I'll be back soon.'

The sun filtered through the leaves. Birds chirped as Shay stirred, woken by the smell of baking bread. She would miss this the most. Even the bread from the castle kitchen at home didn't taste as good. Throwing back her blanket, she saw that Devlin's side was empty. Wealdrun had spent an hour or so alone with Devlin the night before, and she knew that her brother was also now ready to leave this morning.

As she climbed from the hammock, laughter floated across from the campfire. Devlin was seated around the cooking fire with his Culchan friends. There was smiling Ailpain, with his flash of white streaking through dark green hair, and

Fearghus, tallest of the group. Beside them was Reaghan, impulsive and wild. His thick, coppery green plaits shone in the morning sun.

'Good morning,' Devlin said, lifting his head from the mug of steaming tea. 'I'm packed,' he said confidently. "Are you ready?'

She looked at him and smiled. Was this the same Devlin she had left home with?

'As soon as I've had something to eat,' she said, sitting on a tree stump next to Fearghus. 'And packed my bag.'

He handed her a slab of warm bread dripping with melted butter, and they ate in silence, both now thinking of the task ahead.

CHAPTER
10

Half an hour later, they were ready. A sled was loaded with snowshoes of woven birch and their shields, also supplies of dried meat, nuts and fruit. With bow and arrows strapped to their backs, and swords hanging from leather belts, they farewelled their friends and followed Wealdrun along the stream, pulling the sled over soft grass.

They came to a narrow entrance between two high cliffs. Ferns grew from crevices in crags and sharp stones covered the path. The stream narrowed to a trickle, and the light disappeared. Devlin thought that if he stretched out both arms he could touch the sides of the ravine and feel the water trickling onto the ground. It was cold, a frozen silence charging the air. They stopped to wrap themselves in their cloaks, once again pulling their hoods around their faces.

'It will be even colder once you leave the pass,' Wealdrun said. 'This is where I must leave you.' He pointed to a narrow opening, barely visible between a stand of trees. 'Beyond the trees is the entrance into the Frozen Northlands. I can go no further. Culchans are not winter people. The dark is a cold, impenetrable barrier; it has always been for us.'

Both Shay and Devlin were suddenly filled with dread at the thought of entering the unknown world of the Dark Lord and his army of the undead.

Wealdrun, sensing their fear, held them close, wrapped in the warmth of his body. 'Be safe,' he whispered as he released them from his embrace. 'Your father waits for you.'

'Let's go,' Devlin said.

'Will we see you again?' Shay asked Wealdrun, holding back tears.

'When the time comes we may meet again. Until then follow the path laid out for you.' He turned and shuffled back into the mist without a backward glance.

'Let's go,' Devlin said again, picking up the thick rope attached to the sled.

They trod warily from the narrow pass and into a valley surrounded by rugged mountains. Snow clung to the sharp needles of dark pines and the rim of a distant volcano glowed red, lighting up the dark skies.

Snow begun to fall like small shards of ice, driving the sharp flakes into their cheeks. They pulled their hoods low over their eyes and struggled on through rising snowdrifts, dragging the sled across the soft snow, around rocky outcrops.

'At least the sand was warm,' Devlin muttered as he pulled the scarf tight around his frozen face.

'But we won't die of thirst,' Shay retorted.

'There's the track we want,' Devlin said when they finally reached the far side of the valley and faced a narrow track winding up into the mountains. 'Wealdrun gave me all the directions we need.'

They climbed for hours, munching nuts and stopping only to drink. A cold, biting wind howled across the snow, cutting through their bodies. The snow continued to fall and with each step the sled grew heavier and heavier. Eventually they reached a patch of flat land.

'We're on top of the mountains,' Shay whispered, fearing her voice would echo across the snow and wondering if Devlin had seen the dark shadows tracking their every move. She remained silent, her fingers around the amber stone, comforted by its sudden warmth.

'Did you hear that?' Devlin whispered. 'There's

something in the trees.'

'It's just the wind. It's too cold for anything else. Birds would freeze to death.' Shay remained unwilling to admit that she had also seen the sinister shapes darting between the treetops. 'Anyway, we're at the peak, the snow's getting heavier and the sky is already turning black. We have to find somewhere safe, out of the wind.'

'There are some big rocks over there,' Devlin said, pointing to a rocky outcrop shaped like a broken circle. Banks of snow behind the rocks had created a small hollow in the centre circle. 'We can sling the sled cover across two of the rocks, make a tent and sleep inside on the sled. You can collect some of those broken branches and make a fire.'

Shay opened her cloak and pulled out a small pouch. 'Something to warm us.'

By the time they finished the dark had settled. Inside the shelter they huddled on the sled, sipping the hot tea and listening to the wail of the wind outside as it crashed through the trees.

Devlin woke with a start. 'What was that?' He sat up and felt at his side for Shay. She was gone. 'Shay, where are you?' he shouted above the screech of the wind.

'Out here.'

He heard her voice outside and peeled back the cover. 'What are you doing? It's freezing out there.'

'Didn't you hear them?' Shay said. 'They were wailing and screeching. I thought it was the wind, or maybe even wolves, and then they flew into the side of the shelter.'

'What? What are you talking about?'

'The Brendts. They're here. They've followed us. It wasn't the wind you heard in the trees. I saw them and now they have almost ripped the cover open. But I stopped them,' Shay said. Her eyes were glazed and the corners of her lips turned up with a smile.

Devlin began to speak, tripping over his words.

'What are you talking about?'

'Don't ask,' Shay replied, holding up her hand.

'It's better that you don't know. Anyway, they've gone and the wind has settled. Let's get going. We don't know how much further we have to go.'

Dull morning light shaded the clearing as they packed the sled. Something caught Devlin's eye on the largest of the stones around them. He wandered across the soft snow and ran his fingers across the pale red surface.

'Shay,' he called. 'Look at this. What does it remind you of?'

She finished tying down the cover before joining him. 'What? We don't have time to sightsee!'

'These,' Devlin said, pointing to markings etched into the stone. 'They're just like the ones on the sentinel.'

'And the tapestries,' Shay replied. 'Almost everything has been on the tapestries. The sentinel, the mountains and the volcano.'

'You're right,' Devlin said. 'Remember the tapestry above the fireplace in the Great Hall, the little people hiding behind some trees. Think about it. They must have been the Culchans.'

'But that's where it all ended. There are no more tapestries. Mother and the other women started a new panel, but stopped when the army left. Maybe we'll be in the last panel when we return home with Father,' Shay said hopefully, looking at Devlin as he returned to the sled and dragged it across the clearing.

They continued the journey. The feeble morning sun struggled through the dark clouds, but at least the snow and wind of the previous day had receded.

'How much longer?' Shay said wearily as they climbed a steep slope. The sky was turning black, merging with the dark clouds. 'I don't know how much longer I can pull this sled, and I'm sure the Brendts are tailing us again. Did you hear them?'

'Yes, I did,' Devlin said. 'But the further we go the smaller the trees seem to be. Maybe that's why they haven't attacked. The trees are too small for them. The map showed the citadel on a plateau between two mountains, and we must be close.'

'Are you sure?' she replied. 'Every time we reach a peak there's another one waiting for us.'

Devlin shrugged his shoulders and grabbed hold of the rope and pulled the sled as the snow began to fall again and the wind rose once more.

CHAPTER
11

The day stretched out as they tramped across the dark, frozen landscape, half blinded by the unrelenting snow, and on the constant lookout for Brendts. They continued on, their snowshoes sinking into soft snowdrifts, and the wind growing stronger and even colder. Finally they crested a steep ridge. The snow ceased and they looked down onto a sheet of ice rising above a swirling mist. A fresh flurry of snowflakes floated down from the storm clouds.

'That must be the glacier,' Devlin said as he brushed the snow from his face. 'It's the same as the drawing on the map. The citadel can't be far now. And there's the ice wall!' he added in excitement, pointing to a jagged dam of ice towering through the swirling mist. The ice rose from a frozen lake in long sharp slivers, like icy fingers grasping for the dark clouds circling overhead.

A flash of blue lightning illuminated the scene, and they could see how the ice wall stretched across part of the frozen lake, almost blocking out the mountains behind it.

'And there's Drepe's citadel!' Devlin shouted, pointing to towers of ice just visible beyond the wall, almost scratching the low, dark sky on the far side of the lake. 'It has to be. The map showed it on the edge of the lake.'

They slipped and slid down the dangerous, narrow path until they reached the base of the glacier where it entered the lake of ice. Black trees, leaning ominously in on each other, edged around the base of the Ice Citadel where it rose from a rocky ledge. Flames flickered in its narrow windows, casting dancing silhouettes across the frozen surface of the lake.

Shay put her hand to her mouth, stifling a cry. 'The shadows, Devlin . . . What can you see?'

More lightning lit up the sky and Devlin saw them. 'Soldiers and horses,' he cried. 'We've found them. We've found the Red army!'

He picked up a heavy branch, ran at the wall and began to batter at it, harder and harder, until he sank exhausted to the ground. 'It's too hard. We'll never get them out.' He fought back tears as he lifted the branch again and pounded once more against the thick ice.

Shay put her hand on his shoulder.

'Put it down. You know what we have to do.' Her thoughts went back to the lessons with her mother, and the guidance of Wealdrun. 'We have to enter the citadel.'

She took hold of his hand, then clasped the turquoise stone. A white glow encircled them and a warm wind wrapped around them like a soft blanket, lifting and tossing their bodies on swirling gusts. As the wind paused, they opened their eyes and stumbled as their feet landed on a patch of uneven cobblestones in the centre of a courtyard. A flurry of light snow fell at their feet.

'We're here,' Shay whispered to herself. 'We made it.'

'Hide!' Devlin hissed at his sister. 'Get back, over here.' He grapped Shay's hand and pulled them both into a shadowy crevice against the wall dotted with small windows and one entrance. From here, they stared through a gap in the stone at a larger courtyard on the other side.

Flaming torches hung from metal brackets driven into the thick ice of the battlements and ghostly figures swathed in heavy cloaks guarded the frozen walls and a heavily-bolted gate. Each man carried a long sword strapped to his body, and a tall spear honed to a jagged, razor-sharp point. Snarling black hounds the size of small ponies padded at the feet of their unearthly masters. In the darkness a thick canopy of green leaves swathed a tall oak standing in the centre of the courtyard. Black limbs branched out like thick arms stretching across the cobbled square.

'Look at that tree, Devlin,' Shay pointed. 'There's no snow on it, or underneath it.'

A chill ran through them as they stared at the tree. A noose hung from a low branch, swaying in the wind and suddenly a dark shadow flew out from the tree and a strong wind blasted across the courtyard.

Devlin looked up as the shadow turned into a Brendt, lifted its heavy wings and circled into the dark sky. Then he remembered: he knew where he had seen the creature before. It had been hovering in the corner of the largest tapestry in the Great Hall of Rosemerta Castle: a strange, bird-like creature with razor-sharp talons, soaring above an army of black knights.

He had thought it was a touch of fantasy from

the person who had embroidered the tapestry. But now he shuddered as he wondered how many more scary images from the tapestries might prove to be true.

CHAPTER 12

Devlin nervously shifted his gaze from the tree. 'We're inside the citadel walls,' he said in amazement. 'How did we get here?'

'The wind brought us,' Shay replied. Her eyes blinked in the flickering light. 'Wealdrun told me the turquoise would lead us to the Stones.'

She fingered the blue stone, feeling calm and controlled. She heard the clear voices of her mother and Wealdrun patiently explaining the purpose of each stone and now, at last, she understood the power of the lessons.

'The turquoise bead, the colour of the sky, controls the wind, the air . . . even thoughts floating in the breeze. The most dangerous of all. Use it wisely.

'Beware of the red. It belongs to a world of fire and flames; a treacherous helper and fearsome teacher. Keep it close.

'The amber is the earth, supporting you in times of need, protecting the wearer from evil. But, beware; it is as fragile as the forests that gave it life. Take great care.

'Black is different; the scariest bead.'

The words faded and she intuitively grasped the amber bead and tried to focus as they crept across the cobblestones. Thick black smoke curled from tall chimneys, casting menacing shadows across the courtyard as they slipped through a narrow doorway and stood at the foot of twisting stone stairs. Roars of men, and the howling of dogs, filled the citadel.

Devlin held his finger to his lips as he took Shay's hand and they silently climbed the stairs.

The sounds grew louder.

At the top, they faced another door. Devlin gripped the handle and cautiously pulled it open. He felt Shay's breath on his neck as they tiptoed through the doorway. The smell of peat and smoke filled the air. They were in a small alcove. Creeping across the floor, they peered over the lip of a low wall, down into the Great Hall of the citadel. The stench of rotting straw filled their nostrils. Grimy trays of putrid food lay on long wooden trestles and men and dogs fought for scraps.

A massive man sprawled in front of a roaring fire. Long black hair hung in loose greasy strands. His eyes glowed in the reflection of the coiling flames as he raised a golden goblet to his lips. Wine dribbled down the sides of his mouth, and into his tangled, filthy beard.

'That must be Drepe,' Devlin said, recalling the Dark Lords of the past in the tapestries: images showing black wolfskin cloaks wrapped around their bulky bodies, with leering wolf heads topping the cloaks like black crowns.

'Look at his chair,' Shay whispered. 'It's covered in bones.' A bleached skull sat at the top of the high-backed chair and purple sapphires glowed from its sunken eye sockets.

Drepe stood, stretching out his thick hairy arms which were entwined with armbands of writhing silver snakes.

'I smell danger!' he roared.

A black-clothed shape stepped from the shadows and knelt at his feet. 'Sire, you have nothing to fear,' he said. 'You have the Stones. You have defeated the Red army. The boy is dead. There is no one left to challenge you. No one to fear. The Stones are yours.'

Shay and Devlin shrank back, aghast. The kneeling man was their brother Siarl! He truly was a servant of the Dark Lord.

Drepe glared at the spindly man. 'Demon's Tree waits for those who do not value their lives. If you wish to hang from the tree, never utter those words in my presence again. I fear no one. And the Stones are safe, locked in the chest.' He pounded his hand on a metal chest next to the Skull Throne. 'No one will challenge me for them. And you will protect them for me,' he roared as he pushed the chest beneath the iron-covered throne.

'Your hellhounds and your spirit-caller help me to protect the chest,' the man in black hissed. 'And no one has ever broken through the walls of the citadel.'

'No one ever will,' Drepe roared. 'Now, bring me more wine.'

A ghostly leather-clad man slunk out from behind the throne. His cruel eyes bore into Siarl's back as the traitorous knight sidled out of the hall, Devlin and Shay looked at each other and Devlin pointed to the stairwell.

'We have found the Luchair Stones,' he whispered. 'And Siarl is with the Dark Lord.'

Shay peered down into the smoky hall. 'If Siarl is guarding the Stones, then we have to get past him. We must have them if we are to free the army. I know this.'

'We must act now,' Devlin whispered. 'Shay, can you use those stones of yours in any way to help me get to that chest?'

'The black . . .' Shay murmured back. 'If I use the black, I can send shadows into the minds of those below. It will build on their terrors, send them chasing enemies who do not exist.' She bent her head, fearful of what she was about to do but determined to do the best she could, then she closed her eyes, breathed deeply and uttered the words of the stone: 'Keep us safe, make us strong.'

A clamour of voices from below suddenly filled the air.

'Intruders!' a voice shouted. 'My lord, we are being attacked!'

Devlin peered over the balcony. The hellhounds were scrambling out from beneath the trestles, their noses twitching in the foul air as their black hackles rose up from gaunt backbones. They sniffed the air as they loped, growling and snarling, across the hall until they reached the doors. Drepe's men followed with swords drawn. Their feet pounded on the flagstones.

Devlin glanced at Shay. She had her eyes shut, all her attention concentrated on her necklace. He would have to get the chest on his own! He drew his sword and sneaked down the steps until he saw an entrance into the hall. Just as he took a deep breath, Drepe lumbered to his feet, unsheathed his sword and stamped across the hall. 'Bring me the intruders!' he roared. 'Do I have to do everything myself?'

The hall emptied as men and beasts rushed out, leaving behind only a deathly silence. Devlin moved silently over to the Skull Throne. He knelt and reached beneath, feeling for the chest. He grasped the chest and pulled it out. It was heavy, but he managed to hoist it in his arms and stagger up the steps again. He sat against the wall, gasping for air.

Shay was quickly at his side. It had worked! They had the chest, but not much time. Each reached for an iron ring at either end of the chest, then they heaved it into a small room and closed the door.

They heard Drepe return to the hall, roaring at his men. 'There is nothing here, or outside. The hounds are jumping at shadows. Where is my wine?' he bellowed, slumping back onto his throne.

A guard rushed into the hall. 'Lord,' he called as he grovelled breathlessly at the foot of the throne. 'The citadel has been breached. I saw two children from the shadows of Demon's Tree. But I know not where they went.' He kept his head pressed against the hard floor, afraid to look into the eyes of Drepe.

The Dark Lord threw out his leg and the man sprawled in the filthy straw. 'Children?' he shouted. 'It is mere children who have caused this uproar?'

'The chest, my lord, where is the chest?' one of his men cried out. 'The chest has been stolen!'

Drepe rose to his feet, his hand on his sword. 'It cannot be far. The chest must still be inside the walls of the citadel. The thieves will never get past the guards. Find it!' he howled.

'The forests,' one of his men shouted. 'That's where the intruders intruders came from. They must be trying to escape that way.'

'Go then,' Drepe thundered. 'But I want the thieves alive. They will suffer as none has ever suffered before. Prepare Demon's Tree. Do not return without the intruders." And then, with a final bellow, 'Lock all entrances behind you.'

The ghostly men hammered the winged hilts of their swords on the wooden benches and chanted a war cry that shook the icy walls. Hellhounds, their sharp teeth bared in their rush for the taste of blood, followed as the Dark army rushed from the hall. Drepe remained slumped on his throne.

Shay and Devlin stared at the chest. A large iron padlock hung from the lid. Devlin wondered how they would be able to open it without the keys, but Shay smiled softly. Instinct gave her the answer.

She reached for her beads again, held the warming ruby to her heart and closed her eyes as she held the lock with her other hand. She saw her father riding his white charger through the gates of Rosemerta Castle. The path was lined with cheering people as he led the army beneath the portcullis and across the courtyard to the steps of the Keep where her mother waited.

'Come to me, come to us,' she whispered.

The lock warmed in her hand. A voice murmured in her head, 'Do not be afraid. I will come to you. The Red army will rise from the ice.'

She opened her eyes. Devlin was looking at her in amazement. The lock was shuddering. Devlin wrenched at the lock, but the chest would not open.

'Again!' He urgenced Shay. 'Do what you did again." But the lock wouldn't budge. As Devlin wrestled with at the lock, he noticed a familar pattern, faded and barely visable, etched around the edges lock. He traced the lines with his finger tips.

'Devlin, we don't have time for markings!' Shay hissed at brother.

'My sword,' Devlin wispered. 'My sword has the same...' He drew his sword before he finished his sentence. He raised his sword high before gliding the tip of the blade into the lock. There was no mistaking the heavy clunk.

Devlin threw the lock to the ground and lifted the lid of the heavy chest. A soiled bundle of cloth lay at the bottom. As he removed the stained cloth, six black stones shimmered, highlighting a set of spiral symbols carved into their smooth sides.

'The Luchair Stones are red,' he said. 'These are black. We've come all this way for nothing.'

'Look closely.' Shay leaned over his shoulder and peered at the Stones. 'There are flickers of red in the black. Something is happening.'

'The Stones know us,' Devlin said in a whisper

as he realized the truth of her words.

'They know they are going home,' said Shay. 'They turned as black as Drepe while he held them in his power.'

They heard soft footsteps creeping along the corridoor.

'Shay! You must take Stones,' Devlin wispered. 'You have powers to escape from here that I do not have alone.'

'Devlin, I won't leave you.'

'You must.' He said gently but firmly. 'Here.' He thrust the unwrapped Stones into Shay's hands and clasped his hands around hers. 'You must do this for all of us. Now run!'

She buried the Stones in the inside lining of her cloak and turned on her heals toward the door of the room. But the door opened before her hand had clasped the handle.

Siarl towered above them, a burning torch in his hands and rage on his face.

'I would stop there, little sister.' The corners of his mouth turned upwards into a menacing smile.

'You don't need her,' said Devlin, controlling his voice as best he could. 'I believe these are what you're after'. His hand felt for the Stones' stained cloth, poking out of his bretches.

'We have taken them once and we will take them again,' snarled his brother.

'You will not take them back again, Siarl,' he said. 'What has happened to you?' He pulled his sword from its scabbard and stood bravely in front of his older brother. Siarl laughed.

'I have no choice. It was meant to be,' he said. 'The Dark Lord holds my soul. Now you, little brother, will die.'

'Shay, run!' She gasped in horror but turned and fled, pulling her cloak tightly around her as she went.

CHAPTER
13

Siarl raised his weapon, a broadsword of razor-sharp bronze. The blade hissed through the air. Devlin stepped back, slipping on the stone floor. He rolled beneath a trestle.

'I see you fight just like our brother,' Siarl sneered. 'Aled always was a coward.'

Devlin stood up, wide-eyed with fear.

'Hold your sword low and swing up.' His uncle's words filled his head. 'You won't always be training.' He grasped the black sword with both hands as his body trembled. Courage swelled in Devlin. His brother was no longer invincible.

Siarl thrust forward with his sword and came round the bench. Instinctively Devlin ducked and weaved as the sharp edge of his brother's sword swept across the top of his head. 'I'm not finished with you,' Siarl said as they continued to circle each other. He snarled like a wolf, his dark eyes hard and flinty.

Devlin ducked beneath the raised sword and kicked out at a stool, sending it sprawling at Siarl's feet. He stood, legs wide, still grasping his sword hilt with both hands, and pointed it at Siarl's chest.

Siarl growled as he struggled to his feet. Devlin saw the opportunity. He lunged and felt the black sword come to life in his hands. Siarl swung wildly as Devlin lifted his sword. The weapons clashed, metal on metal, and sparks soared as Siarl's broadsword flew from his hand. He stumbled backward through the open door. Devlin lunged as his brother scrambled to his feet.

Siarl held up his arms. 'Well done, little brother. Uncle has trained you well.' He gasped as he lowered his head and charged.

Devlin stepped sideways as Siarl tumbled down the steps. With sweaping precision, Devlin brought his blade down hard enough to remove the giant key hanging from a leather belt around Siarl's waist. It shot across the floor and Devlin reached the key just before Siarl, who, back on his feet, advanced slowly on Devlin who was forced backwards down a passage at the side of the Great Hall. Out of the corner of his eye he noticed swirls of white and turquoise around the locked entrance. And then he saw his opportunity.

Devlin moved into the small anteroom off the passage. Siarl charged at his turned the corner and Devlin ducked through Siarl's legs. There were advantages to being smaller, he thought. As Siarl spun round, he held out his sword, pressing it against his brother's chest, nicking his leather armour as he pushed him further into the tiny room. With one quick movement he kicked the door closed, grasped the heavy iron latch and bolted it down.

'Aled is no coward. He will always win against you,' Devlin yelled as he raced the door. The lock yielded quickly to the giant key that Devlin turned with all his might. He crossed beneath the shadow of Demon's Tree, and out beyond the unguarded castle gates where he followed the path to the lake, away from the malevolence of the citadel and the sounds of the Dark army crashing through the ice in their fruitless search for the intruders.

★★★★★

Shay crouched at the base of the towering wall of ice: a massive frozen barrier. But she seemed to know what to do, almost as if an inner voice was giving her instructions. With a glance over her shoulder to check no one had followed her, she pulled the Stones free of their bag and placed them at the foot of the wall.

Pale rays of red light spluttered from the black heart of the Stones and the ice began to glow and hum.

A soft light flickered in the frozen wall and the ice now began to crack. The Stones were almost fully red by now, coming alive as they threw off their enforced darkness.

Devlin rushed up and knelt at her side. 'It's working,' he whispered.

'Siarl?' Shay asked, fearing the answer.

'Locked up where he cannot harm us,' Devlin said.

'Did you hurt...?' she murmured as she reached out and touched his arm.

'There was no bloodshed. How could there be, between brothers? And now, let us welcome Father and Aled!'

Shards of heavy ice were now tumbling down and the earth shook. Through the ice Shay and Devlin could hear cheering, and see the golden banners of Rosemerta being raised once more: the Red Dragon encircled by six red stones.

The Red army broke free from their frozen prison. The deafening sound of shattering ice shook the ground. The Red Dragon glimmered on the shields of a hundred armoured knights as they rode on whinnying horses, stamping on the unfamiliar soil. Misty coils of breath hung in the air around their flaring nostrils. The dragon flag flew boldly from the tall lances of the rows of archers.

'There must be over a thousand men,' Shay said as they watched the cheering men march past.

Lord Padraig, riding his white charger, lifted his visor and laughed to the knights at his side as the melting ice flowed into the lake.

He looked at his children. 'My beloved youngest children. I knew you would come.' He leaned down and lifted Shay onto his horse, while his oldest son, Aled, who was riding at his father's side, stepped forward and put his hand out to Devlin.

'How did you know we would make it? Siarl left us for dead. He said he had a message from you, but he lied. He led us into danger.' The words tumbled from Shay as she leaned back into her father's arms.

'Siarl doesn't understand,' Padraig said as he ruffled her curls. 'He has chosen his master, but one day, I pray, he will realize that he must come back to us. Now, however, we must face the forces of the Dark Lord one last time.' He stood in the stirrups, turned to the army and raised his sword.

'The Dark army waits for us. We have the Stones!'

The knights stood tall in their stirrups, archers raised their long bows and the valley filled with cheers. Padraig raised his arm.

'Wait, Father,' Devlin whispered. 'I have something to give you.' He pulled a letter from his jerkin and passed it to his father. 'Mother gave it to me as we left the castle. She said that it should be the first thing you saw when you were free.'

Padraig read the letter then turned to Aled.

'The Dark Lord must wait,' he called. 'Men of Rosemerta, we must ride for the Strait of Tremors and Aarush.'

He turned to Shay. 'The Lady Bedwynn tells me that while we have the Stones, Rosemerta will flourish again. The seeds will sprout and there will be a harvest once more.'

Shay nodded. 'I know,' she said softly. 'The Stones have told me so.'

'Why do we have to go to Aarush? What does Mother say?' Aled leaned across, confused. Padraig passed him the letter. He read the words and felt dark shadows curling around his body. Then he straightened in the saddle and turned to the army.

'We ride!' he called. 'Lord Padraig speaks true. We cannot go home yet. The evil awakes in Aarush. We must ride to their rescue!' He turned to the citadel and raised his sword.

'You were right, brother Siarl. It is not a game, and it never will be.'